D1491223

SPECIAL MESSAGE TO READERS

THE ULVERSCROFT FOUNDATION
(registered UK charity number 264873)

was established in 1972 to provide funds for research, diagnosis and treatment of eye diseases. Examples of major projects funded by the Ulverscroft Foundation are:-

- The Children's Eye Unit at Moorfields Eye Hospital, London
- The Ulverscroft Children's Eye Unit at Great Ormond Street Hospital for Sick Children
- Funding research into eye diseases and treatment at the Department of Ophthalmology, University of Leicester
- The Ulverscroft Vision Research Group, Institute of Child Health
- Twin operating theatres at the Western Ophthalmic Hospital, London
- The Chair of Ophthalmology at the Royal Australian College of Ophthalmologists

You can help further the work of the Foundation by making a donation or leaving a legacy. Every contribution is gratefully received. If you would like to help support the Foundation or require further information, please contact:

THE ULVERSCROFT FOUNDATION
The Green, Bradgate Road, Anstey
Leicester LE7 7FU, England
Tel: (0116) 236 4325

website: www.foundation.ulverscroft.com

THE PRINCE'S BRIDE

One of three royal brothers in the Adriatic principality of San Michele, Prince Jonas works hard. But after a protocol-ridden evening, he's due some downtime in his beloved forest. Hope Kennard was the daughter of the manor back in England. But she has guarded her heart since her childhood ended in financial scandal. She's just passing through San Michele, before moving on to another country, another job. But then a charming forest ranger appears. And this time, her instincts don't help . . .

SOPHIE WESTON

THE PRINCE'S BRIDE

Complete and Unabridged

LINFORD
Leicester

First published in Great Britain in 2017

First Linford Edition
published 2018

Copyright © 2017 by Sophie Weston
All rights reserved

A catalogue record for this book is available
from the British Library.

ISBN 978–1–4448–3783–4

Published by
F. A. Thorpe (Publishing)
Anstey, Leicestershire

Set by Words & Graphics Ltd.
Anstey, Leicestershire
Printed and bound in Great Britain by
T. J. International Ltd., Padstow, Cornwall

This book is printed on acid-free paper

1

His Serene Highness Prince Jonas of San Michele was not taking calls. He had been in his office since dawn, working on a contract to satisfy the law firm's most difficult client. And he was not going to stop until all parties had signed up.

His assistants knew the signs. No lunch then. They sent out for sandwiches and told the palace that they would pass on all messages as soon as he was free.

By the time the contract arrived back in the office with both sets of signatures on it, Jonas had biro stains on his shirt, his hair was all over the place, and the afternoon was nearly gone. He didn't care. He went into the outer office, incandescent with pleasure. 'We did it!'

The collective sigh of relief was more eloquent than a standing ovation. People high-fived one another, and someone opened a bottle of San Michele's answer to French champagne. Jonas, Royal Patron of the San Michele Winemakers' Association, laughed and applauded.

'Congratulations. You must be pleased,' murmured the senior paralegal as conversation became general.

'Thank you,' said Jonas. The man had worked for Reval Partners since Jonas's grandfather's time. 'We did a really good job, I think. Don't see how we could have done anything better, anyway. And we had just enough luck to swing it.'

'Group hug?' said the paralegal, a cynic.

Several people groaned and someone said, 'Rather have a group celebratory dinner.'

Jonas shook his head sadly. When he first came back from the States, he had gone out with the team several times after they'd closed a big case. This last year, however, more and more royal duties had intervened. He hadn't even made the Christmas party. 'Sorry, guys.

Not tonight. I need to clean up and head off to the palace for the crown princess's party.'

That reminded them of the messages. A junior unearthed the file and sent it to his phone. He studied it. Between phone calls and emails, there were eleven from assorted officials.

'Ouch,' said Jonas. 'What on earth's going on? I'm not even late yet. I need further and better particulars here.'

He went back into his office, pondering which of his callers to consult. The obvious candidate was the crown princess's personal assistant. But she would say whatever Crown Princess Anna told her to, and his sister-in-law was a micro-manager of other people's time. He decided his best bet was an old friend.

The head of palace security answered his phone with a cheery, 'Hi there!' The head of palace security didn't do cheery, especially when he was on duty.

Jonas blinked. '*Hi there?* You don't fool me, evil alien invader. Let me speak to the real Fredrik Jensson.'

'Good to hear from you,' said Count Fredrik, with only the slightest suggestion of gritted teeth.

'You're not alone, I take it?'

'Not at all. I — ' His voice became fainter as he spoke to someone in the room with him. 'Please reassure Her Serene Highness that Prince Jonas will be here in time for the sunset cocktails. Yes, I'm certain.'

Jonas had a twinge of conscience. 'Sunset cocktails?'

'Have you read *any* of your briefing notes?' said Count Fredrik in quite a different voice, clearly relieved of his previous inhibiting companion.

'Been rather busy at work. But the party is in the diary and I'm on my way. Well, nearly on my way. Need to tidy up a bit first.' Just as well that the always impeccably tailored Fredrik couldn't see him, Jonas thought, amused.

'Good of you to let me know.' The count didn't sound one little bit grateful.

4

Jonas grinned. 'Don't mention it, old friend.'

'Where are you?'

'The office. I'll have a quick shower and — '

'You took your uniform to work, then?'

'Uniform?' Jonas had a sudden cold feeling that he'd missed something major. He wore military uniform on state occasions and forest ranger uniform when he was volunteering in the San Michele forest. He didn't think Fredrik was talking about the rangers.

'But this isn't a state occasion. It's just a cocktail party Anna has arranged for some trade mission, with me filling in for Carlo. Isn't it?'

'Well, that's how it started out,' said Count Fredrik. 'Been a fair few adjustments along the way.'

Jonas groaned. 'I just put it in the diary when Carlo told me he'd be travelling and I'd have to host the thing for Anna. And then forgot about it. What can I do?'

Count Fredrik relented. 'Thought so. I've borrowed you a uniform from the Hussars. Bring your stuff and change here. Grab a cab *now*. I'll meet you by the old stables.'

The old stables currently constituted the palace recycling centre. They were situated at the back of the kitchen complex. 'By the trash cans? Very cloak and dagger.'

Count Fredrik was patient. 'Just get here. Fast as you can.'

But there were no cabs. As the sliding doors of the impressive building swished together behind him, Jonas realized that he was facing a wall of Friday-evening traffic. A stationary wall. It was grid-locked all the way to the main drag. And when he looked up, he saw a queue of vehicles along the steep cobbled way that led to the ancient castle gateway. The cars on the hill weren't moving either.

Jonas stared. This was more than normal Friday-night traffic. He began to wonder just how big this bash of Anna's was. A trade mission didn't normally bring Liburno to a standstill.

'Hell!'

Of course, it was partly his own fault, he acknowledged. If he had employed a social secretary, as his sister-in-law kept nagging him to do, everything would have been taken care of. Someone would have read all those additional emails, if he'd lobbed them into a pending file for when he had the time to catch up.

But Jonas had been saying no to a social secretary ever since he came back from the States. Just like he said no to an apartment in the palace and to a regular security detail at official functions. He would fulfil all the tasks that Parliament or his father required of him. He would stand in for his eldest brother, Crown Prince Carlo, when the family asked him to.

But he'd explained his position to the family again and again. He didn't want a royal lifestyle. He didn't want footmen bringing him his post on a silver tray every morning. And he hated the idea of paparazzi invading his hobbies and his holidays.

His brothers said that was reasonable, his grandmother declared it to be wholly his own affair, and his father just grunted. Only his sister-in-law continued to badger him to change his mind. Worse than that, recently she had started to matchmake. But Jonas had promised to deputize for his elder brother at this evening's red-carpet event while Carlo was abroad. So he would forget how tired he was and head for the palace on foot.

Jonas took off his jacket, stuffed it into his backpack, shouldered the bag and set off. He texted Count Fredrik: *Traffic solid. Walking.*

The reply winged back immediately: *Running would be better.*

After three hours' sleep last night? He'd been working for fifteen hours already.

A second ping: *On parade on the battlements at sunset, remember.*

He broke into a jog, texting as he went. *When's sunset?*

8

Soon.

Jonas took stock. After all, he was young, fit, and he was supposed to be a problem-solver. To get to the old stables, he would normally head up the hill and slip into the park by one of the side gates, where the officer on duty would recognize him. But that would email running past all those stationary cars and limousines, with all the great photo opportunities for bored passengers to snap the fifth in the princely succession panting up late to the evening's royal event. He could just imagine what the crown princess would say to publicity like that.

The alternative was to head into the public park. It was separated from the palace grounds by a stone curtain wall and some serious locked gates, but there was a small entrance that the tree surgeons used, which was usually unlocked during daylight hours.

Jonas broke into a run. Of course, when he got there, the tree surgeons' entrance was locked and bolted. But by now the adrenaline had kicked in. There was a big oak tree by that gate. He had climbed it many times as a boy.

He flung his backpack over the wall and started to climb.

Jonas arrived at the rendezvous with scuffed shoes, a three-cornered rent in his trousers, and hands and face so grubby that any schoolboy tearaway would have accorded him instant respect. He was grinning from ear to ear.

Count Fredrik was pacing impatiently in front of the portico of the old stables. 'What happened?' he demanded, turning towards the palace and urging Jonas into a near-run.

'Had to climb over the fence. Somebody had locked the gate.'

The head of security grunted but didn't slacken his pace. He shot them round the corner of the eighteenth-century kitchen wing to an anonymous door, and fished out a key.

'Back stairs?' said Jonas knowledgeably.

'Naturally.'

The count urged him through the door, then locked and bolted it behind them. He checked his watch. 'First you change. Then you hit the battlements for the sunset cocktails. You've got less than half an hour.'

'Change? What am I, Spiderman?'

The Reval brothers and Fredrik had taken Jonas's young nephew to an all-day Spiderman marathon just before Christmas. A faint smile twitched the corner of Count Fredrik's firm mouth at last. 'Full military uniform.'

'*What?*'

'With sword.'

'You're joking.'

'I never joke on duty,' said the count, and hustled him into the old tack room.

Jonas saw that it had been set up with long trestle tables. People sat at them, studying screens. Nobody took any notice of the new arrivals. Jonas peered over one woman's shoulder and saw that she was watching glamorous guests at the foot of the palace's grandest staircase. She was wearing an earpiece with a tiny microphone attached.

'Wow,' he said, genuinely startled. 'Real-time surveillance. Who's here?'

'Hollywood A-listers and money,' the count told him crisply. 'You can change through there.'

And no, he hadn't been joking. The white dress uniform of the San Michele Hussars, with epaulettes, gleaming buttons, row of medals and a ceremonial scarlet sash hung on the back of the door of what must once have been a broom cupboard. Someone had added gold-braid aiguillettes.

Jonas stared at it. '*Aiguillettes?*'

'Special request of Crown Princess Anna.' In spite of not joking on duty, Count Fredrik was having difficulty keeping a straight face. 'Look, I found you a uniform, OK? Thank you, Fredrik, for your foresight and efficiency. Not at all, Your Serene Highness, all in a day's work.'

Jonas was contrite. 'I'm really very grateful, Fredrik. Honest. You've saved my bacon.'

'Let's say I've given your bacon a sporting chance.'

The former broom cupboard, though cold, had a businesslike shower and a plentiful supply of towels. Jonas began to wrestle with his stained shirt. A button shot across the room like a bullet. Count Fredrik sidestepped. Jonas gave up on buttons and started to haul the shirt over his head. 'Pass me my pack?' He kicked off his office shoes, then tried to remove one sock with the other foot, failed, and staggered painfully into the wall. He swore under his breath.

'Pack's on the bench,' said his friend helpfully. 'I draw the line at excavating for your underwear.'

Jonas, still muffled, was absorbed in his own struggles.

'You're hopping,' said Count Fredrik dispassionately. 'We have no time for you to hop.'

'How long have we got?'

'Twenty minutes, give or take. Try undoing the shirt cuffs.'

13

'I know. I forgot. Can you please turn on the damn shower? This will only take a minute.'

Count Fredrik trod round him, reached into the shower and swung a dial before stepping smartly away from the water.

'AAARGH!' yelled Jonas, finally dragging the shirt over his head and lobbing it away from him. Count Fredrik caught it on the fly, bundled it up and tossed it onto the growing pile of Jonas's discarded garments.

His Serene Highness flung himself under the spray, muttering. He reached for the shower gel and raised his voice in challenge. 'Has it occurred to you that I could stay here until someone brings me a sensible change of clothing?'

'Define sensible.'

Jonas had no trouble doing that. 'No gold aiguillettes. No medals. What would Anna do then, eh?'

Count Fredrik was unmoved. 'Remind you that you're also two hours late. You haven't done your duty on the receiving line. And you missed the English tea and speeches entirely.'

Jonas gasped, swallowed water, coughed until his eyes watered, and opened the shower door, towelling hard. 'English tea? I don't remember that.'

'It entered the programme about ten days ago.'

'That would account for it. But *why*?'

'You'd have to ask Princess Anna. I just do what I'm told.'

Conscience struck again. 'Oh Lord yes. You should be out there securing something, shouldn't you? Leave me. I can finish up and head for the battlements.'

'My team will alert me if there's anything that needs my attention.'

'But — '

'I'll see you to the starting gate. We're both in enough hot water already.'

'Greater love hath no man than he will stand up to a crown princess for his friend,' said Jonas, moved.

'You'd better believe it.'

Jonas rummaged through his pack for socks and underwear. When he found them, Fredrik stuffed the clutch of discarded clothes into it and zipped it up. 'Thanks. I suppose Anna is really mad at me?'

'Yes.'

'Blast.'

The count passed him a pile of neatly folded undergarments. 'Standard Hussars issue, sourced from the regiment. We're both going to owe those guys.'

The first was not much more than a silk T-shirt. 'At least there are no buttons on this to fly off and take someone's eye out,' said Jonas with satisfaction. 'How's the time going?'

'Fifteen minutes and counting.'

Jonas pulled up the dress trousers, flexed the white braces and pulled them up onto his shoulders. 'Nearly there. No patent leather shoes?' he asked mischievously.

'Gentlemen,' said the count with dignity, 'do not wear patent leather shoes with San Michele Hussar formal dress uniform. Mess boots are correct, ideally well-polished.'

They both looked at Jonas's scuffed footwear. Jonas hauled his torn shirt back out of his pack and rubbed the worst of the soil and twiggery off them. They both considered the result.

'No,' Jonas agreed sadly.

Fredrik produced a pair of pull-on ankle boots in soft black leather, polished so you could see your face in them. 'They may be a little big.'

'Don't worry. I can wade, if I have to.'

'Which is why I've spared you the spurs. *Exceptionally.*'

'Did I say you're a lifesaver, Fredrik?'

Fredrik gave a mock bow, acknowledging the compliment, and handed him the white jacket. Jonas shrugged into it, flexing his arms under the heavy material. The cuffs were stiff, with navy-blue frogging and gold braid. He pulled them down, smoothed each sleeve, and began to do up the brightly polished buttons, fumbling with haste.

The count picked up Jonas's watch

and signet ring and observed him critically. 'Do you want a hand?'

Jonas waved him away. The medals danced and twisted as he wrestled with tight buttonholes and missed. 'Dammit. Why are there so many bloody buttons?'

'Sure you don't want help?'

'Maybe just the top button and the collar.' And, as the count complied, 'God, this jacket is uncomfortable. Where's my watch? Ring?'

Count Fredrik handed them over silently.

'Oh Lord, have you seen the time? Give me that blasted sash and let's get going.'

'Hair?'

Jonas ducked to look in the spotted mirror and ran his fingers through his super-clean hair. It flopped forward, giving him a rakish bartender look that would drive the crown princess crazy. Oh well, she'd have to make do with the rest of the pantomime get-up, he thought. He cast a look of loathing at the shining black leather boots. 'Someone really *worked* to get those sparkling, didn't they?' And before Count Fredrik could reply: 'OK, OK, no more complaining.' He flicked the medals into place, straightened, and threw a mock salute at the image in the mirror. 'Let's go.'

'Good choice. Seven minutes and counting.'

Jonas started to run up the spiral stairs, then slowed. Count Fredrik had been badly wounded on his last tour of duty with the San Michele Army. The injury to his leg had stopped their climbing expeditions. Fredrik had never discussed it and Jonas had never asked. But now he wondered whether pelting up four flights of a spiral staircase in the old tower would cause him pain.

'Shift,' said his friend crisply. Which seemed to answer the question.

Jonas settled the scarlet sash over his head and across his jacket with practised fingers. As they went, Count Fredrik's cell phone beeped. He glanced at the screen. 'The crown princess's PA,' he said briefly.

'Wanting to know where I am.'

'That's the — er — gist of it, yes.'

Jonas laughed but he shook his head too. 'The woman never gives up.' He stopped and turned, holding out an imperative hand. 'Give.'

Count Fredrik did.

Jonas called the number back and said, 'Please tell her Serene Highness that I understood that she wanted me on the battlements. That's where I'm headed right now. Has there been a change of plan?'

The flustered PA said no, she didn't think so.

'Thank you,' said Jonas with gentle courtesy and ended the call. He gave the phone back to the count. 'And now, for the last time this evening, I'm gonna run.'

He powered up the rest of the stairs and made it onto the battlements a good five minutes before the crown princess arrived. Fredrik was not far behind.

Crown Princess Anna came hurrying

along the walkway from the eighteenth-century wing. Her floaty dress flattened itself against her legs in the spring breeze, but her blonde hair was as rigid as a soldier on sentry duty. So was her jaw.

Observing that, Jonas felt his heart sink. He took refuge in determined bonhomie. 'Hi there, Anna. You see — I made it at last.'

She showed her teeth. Even her dearest friend couldn't have called it a smile. 'Lucky me.'

Ah. More contrition needed. 'Really sorry I'm late. Major job in the office that needed closing tonight. Really.'

She pursed her lips, unappeased.

'And I had to clear the desk before my vacation,' Jonas said with just a hint of self-righteousness.

Count Fredrik began, 'The traffic —'

Crown Princess Anna silenced them both with a viciously upraised forefinger. Count Fredrik's face became a mask. He stepped back. She ignored him. Indeed, she hardly seemed to be aware that he was there at all. Horrified at the discourtesy, Jonas half-turned to him, but the princess seized him by the princely sash and rapped out, 'Have you memorized the guests you need to talk to?'

Jonas abandoned bonhomie and contrition alike. Time for some straight talking, he thought. 'No.' For a startled moment, he thought she might even hit him.

She ground her teeth. 'Did you even read your briefing? Don't bother to answer that.' She was already calling up someone on speed dial. 'Celina? Will you be good enough to ask the Grand Duchess if she can spare you, please? Join me on the south battlements as soon as you can.' She ended the call and turned a basilisk stare on Jonas, inspecting him from head to toe. 'At least you're here now. And dressed. We shall just have to — ' She broke off, her eyes narrowing sharply. '*Sword!*'

Jonas chuckled. 'It's a party, Anna, not the state opening of Parliament. I'm not going to be spearing prawn canapés at swordpoint. Why not just forget it? No one will notice, not with all the buttons and braid.'

She rounded on Count Fredrik. 'Where did he leave it?'

The head of security stayed inscrutable. 'I will organize a search.'

'*You*,' said Crown Princess Anna, shaking with temper and not inscrutable at all, 'will go and get it. Now.'

There was a dangerous silence. Then Count Fredrik, expressionless, clicked his heels and went without a word.

All desire to laugh had left. Jonas was cold with anger. He said crisply, 'May I remind you that Fredrik is not only a national hero, he is also the head of palace security, and paid by the state? You can't send him on your damn errands like a pageboy. One, it's discourteous. Two, you're exceeding your authority.'

The crown princess blinked and spluttered as if someone had thrown water over her. 'How dare you?'

'Don't be ridiculous. Of course I dare. What's more, you know perfectly well I'm right.'

She could barely speak. 'You. You. You. No, you're not right. You're not right about anything. You're no use at all. Not to San Michele. Not to the family. You're a parasite and a passenger.' The venom was unmistakable.

Jonas flung up a hand to stop her. But Anna had clearly been working on her sense of grievance for a long time. She launched into a diatribe, part of which she could hardly get out, her words tumbling over each other. But far too much of it had clearly been well rehearsed. He listened, expressionless.

He was irresponsible, selfish and arrogant, she said. He did exactly what he wanted to do, and the hell with anyone else. He had no sense of duty. No appreciation of how lucky he was. Oh, he might have joined the family firm, but he never pretended that he enjoyed it or tried to hide his indifference to practising law.

'Carlo says your heart isn't in it,' she threw at him. She was clearly quoting the crown prince verbatim.

Jonas winced. Carlo was not only his much-loved older brother, he was also head of their legal practice. 'I think you'll find you've said enough.'

But having brooded on her brother-in-law's iniquities for the best part of a busy day, the crown princess was on a roll. She continued in the same vein, shaking her head so violently that her iron-steady hair started to fly with the force of her invective. ' . . . I've been doing my best to interest the international film industry makers in San Michele ever since your father made me head of the film council, and . . . '

Jonas had had enough. 'You're not head of the film council,' he said very quietly. 'You're the royal patron.'

' . . . you do nothing to support me. Nothing.' She stopped dead, staring. 'What do you mean?'

'You know no more about the film industry than I do.' His voice was even but very clear. 'You're just a bossy busybody who likes giving parties that film stars come to. You don't run anything — except everybody else ragged.'

Her mouth moved silently as if she were still yelling at him, though no sound came out.

'You should apologize to Count Fredrik when he returns. And then, for God's sake, get a grip. San Michele doesn't need you running round like a charging heifer, scaring the life out of anyone who might get in your way.'

Before she could find an answer, there was the clip of high heels on the walkway, and his grandmother's assistant hurried round the corner. She was carrying a leather belt with an ornate buckle that he ought already to be wearing. And the sword.

Oh hell and damnation, thought Jonas. He was already beginning to regret letting himself be carried away. Yes, the way Anna had treated Count Fredrik was outrageous. But all he'd needed to do was point that out and let her common sense do the rest. What on earth had possessed him to get into a slanging match with the woman?

And then to have Celina find them glaring at each other like a couple of drunken sailors brawling on the waterfront! Celina! One of the few people in San Michele he felt close to these days. The woman who, if his best friend Jack hadn't seen her first, he would have wined and dined and dated and maybe even married, with a fair wind behind him and a little luck on his side.

He felt ashamed. And that made him even angrier. 'Thank you,' he said savagely, almost wrenching the sword out of Celina's hand. He refused all help, flinging the sword belt round the waist of his jacket and jerking the complicated clasp together with a ferocity that brooked no resistance from mere metal. He settled the red sash ruthlessly back into place and glared round. 'So what do I have to do?'

Celina had brought a list. She looked

uncertainly at the crown princess, but when Anna stayed silent, she consulted it and read, 'Cocktails at sunset on the battlements.' She looked up. 'Actually, the stewards are already herding — I mean directing — the guests this way.'

'*Herding* was just fine,' said Jonas darkly. Anna's look flamed him. He ignored it.

Celina said diplomatically, 'I passed them on the stairs. Siri Fair is the actress to look out for. I'll send drinks over, and then you and she are going to have to stand and chat by the turret wall, so you can be photographed against the setting sun.'

Jonas was speechless. Celina consulted her briefing notes again. 'Her production company is considering making part of her next movie here in Liburno.'

Jonas found his voice. It was deceptively affable. 'So I'm here as a prop in a photo shoot, am I? That explains the sword.'

That broke the crown princess out of

her marble calm. 'For God's sake, don't make a fuss, Jonas.' She sounded really alarmed. 'We needed a Prince Charming tonight. You were the best available.'

There was moment of total disbelief. And then Jonas dropped his head in his hands and laughed helplessly.

2

Life is full of new experiences, thought Hope Kennard.

Three weeks ago she had been on top of the world, managing a ski chalet in the French Alps, working for people she liked and trusted, doing a job she was good at — busy, responsible and competent. Two weeks ago she had been unemployed and homeless; and what was worse, with her capacity for trust in tatters. Again.

And now here she was in the Republic of San Michele, which she had never heard of a week ago, notionally house-sitting but in practice running therapy sessions for a one-girl dog. The (mainly) German shepherd had gone into mourning when his owner, eleven-year-old Poppy Anton, had been swept off on a family sailing holiday. The other family pets had happily gone along too, but Moby — named for Moby Dick, an animal he resembled only in his massive size — was seasick. Hope's role was to exercise him frequently and try to keep his mind off his broken heart.

Moby had melting brown eyes and an unerring sense of direction when it came to the biscuit tin. The family, sailing down the Dalmatian coast, tied up in a different port every evening. And every morning Poppy got up before anyone else in the party, took herself to a café with Wi-Fi, and chatted to Moby over her breakfast.

This morning was no exception. The kitchen laptop thrummed into life. Moby stopped looking at the biscuit tin and jumped onto one of the long kitchen benches in front of it and sat to attention.

Hope leaned across him and tapped the green telephone icon on the screen. At once Moby shoved her aside and barked twice. The screen swirled a bit and then Hope, peering past Moby's massive shoulders, saw freckles, braces on teeth and the unmistakable plaits tilted at an impossible angle.

'Good morning, my lamb,' crooned Poppy.

Moby made crooning noises back.

They talked in their private language until Moby was satisfied. Then he shifted enough to allow Hope to slide onto the bench beside him and see the screen properly.

'Good morning, Hope,' said Poppy, beaming like sunlight.

She'd soon dropped the polite and proper 'Ms Kennard'. These days Poppy and Hope were acknowledged allies. And they worked well together, Hope thought now. She reached for the biscuit tin, ready for their morning ritual.

Poppy waved her croissant in front of her smartphone. Moby's tail began to wag furiously. He put his front paws on the table and gave an imperious short bark. Poppy broke off a corner of the pastry as Hope slid a biscuit out of the tin. Poppy looked off screen right, raised her arm and mimed a throw. Moby leaped off the bench, jumping and giving little barks in his excitement. Hope immediately tossed the biscuit so that it sailed over Moby's head. He turned and raced after it, his claws clicking as he skidded on the polished floor.

Poppy laughed in delight. 'Gets him every time,' she said fondly.

'Very rewarding,' said Hope. She was not just talking about the dog. More and more, Poppy was reminding her of herself as a schoolgirl — too quiet, a little lost, only truly at ease with her beloved animal friend. In Hope's case it had been a pony: fat, contrary and stubborn. He never came when she called; but when he eventually deigned to trot over and accept his bridle, he would nuzzle her hair and blow down her T-shirt. And she'd loved him. Until one day her father decided she had outgrown him and he was sold.

Hope hadn't even had time to say

goodbye. Her father, infuriated by her grief when he was so excited to give her his wonderful present, had refused to discuss that matter. So seven-year-old Hope refused to have anything to do with the larger pony he wanted to buy her. He called it 'the next step'. She called it treachery and went into mourning. Poor Daddy — he'd never understood about love, not even at the end, she thought now. At least Poppy's father, initially dismissive of Poppy's despair at the thought of a bereft Moby, now showed signs of learning.

But neither of her companions noticed the undercurrent. Moby made short work of the biscuit and pounded back to the bench, ears pricked, quivering with anticipation. Poppy and Hope repeated the trick three more times. Only the last time Hope threw his rubber bone instead, and Moby settled down to chew it contentedly in the corner. He never took his eyes off the screen, though.

'Still missing me,' said Poppy, her joy dimming.

'He could do with a longer run,' said Hope. She had never been responsible for a dog before, but her brother Max had two and had sent her a reading list on German shepherds. 'I take him into the woods every day, but it's a bit of a routine. He may be getting bored. A whole day among some new trees would be even better.'

Poppy looked wistful. 'If we were home, Mother would take us into the old forest.'

'Then I can take him into the old forest,' Hope said stoutly. She might not know much about dogs, but she was learning fast; and unlike her fat pony, Moby came when she called.

The little face on the screen was instantly anxious. 'You need a permit. Dad has a family one because he's a volunteer fire ranger, but — '

'Moby *is* family. And I'm in loco parentis, so I'll count too.'

'Are you sure?'

Hope didn't know about the forest by-laws but, in five years of working her way round the world, she had talked herself out of tighter spots than taking a dog into a forest on a *slightly* dodgy permit. 'Yes.'

She saw Poppy allowing herself to believe. 'That would be so great.'

Hope smiled at her. 'Consider it done, then.'

★ ★ ★

The Antons had good maps. Hope found the forest road without difficulty, and Moby barked excitedly as she turned into the parking place. The air tasted as sweet and cold as champagne on ice as they set off, Moby tearing ahead and then racing back to her, almost dancing.

But they came to a small clearing and the dog's mood changed. He ran round, peering behind trees and following small animal tracks, getting more and more frantic. It took Hope a while, but eventually she worked out that he was looking for Poppy and couldn't find her. Her eyes prickled. Ridiculous!

'She'll be back,' she said, knowing it was to comfort herself as much as the dog.

He continued to search for ages. Hope sat down on an old tree stump and waited until he gave up. Eventually he came back, legs dragging, head down, a picture of misery.

'Oh, Moby,' she said. 'I'm so sorry.'

The dog slumped down onto his haunches, put back his head and howled at the sky.

*   *   *

Jonas pushed his motorbike into the barn behind the forest rangers' centre. He had ridden out of Liburno last night in the small hours in a cold rage at Hollywood, San Michele, and most of all himself.

It was not at all what he'd intended. But when he got back to his apartment, he was so restless that he knew he'd never sleep, even though he should be exhausted. So he'd flung a few essentials into the canvas bag that he always took on the bike and set out for the forest. Two weeks of volunteering on forest conservation and a refresher course on fire-watching should be enough to restore his equilibrium. Or at least he hoped so. He felt as if he were in a cage and if he didn't stretch his wings in the air he'd die.

He locked the bike and headed for the rangers' building, where he would be staying for the next two weeks. It was a simple structure: four Spartan bedrooms, a common room for socializing, a command centre for planning and training, and a big display space for educating everyone from tourists to schoolchildren in all aspects of the great European birch forest.

Jonas wondered whether he'd be staying there alone this time. Most of the rangers and nearly all volunteers lived locally. Jonas himself was welcome, because after all his legal qualifications, he'd done a master's degree in wilderness conservation in the States. That meant he'd got practical experience too. Besides, his beloved godfather had been a lifelong ranger. So he had a sort of family ticket, by proxy. But basically the rangers were a close-knit group who regarded the capital as a foreign country and the thirty-seven miles of road between Liburno and the forest as a welcome obstacle to interspecies contamination.

Jonas loved them. Remembering that, he gave a long, grateful sigh. 'Free at last,' he said aloud.

There was nobody in the centre when Jonas let himself in. He saw from the new page on the desk diary that the team captain had signed in around dawn. Jonas chuckled. Taking his state-of-the-art devices to record the dawn chorus, no doubt!

Jonas chose a room in the living quarters and flung his kit bag onto the single bed. The forest beyond the window was alive with movement. Time to go outside and breathe again, he thought. He divested himself of his leathers and dug into the bag for a fleece. The forest would be cooler than Liburno. He pulled it on, grimacing as he accidentally brushed the grated scar at his waist.

That damned belt! He had to take a chisel and a tin opener to the buckle to unlock it, in the end. He'd have to write a letter of apology to the Hussars, whose property it was. And also find some way of making reparation for the insult to the regiment. Noblesse oblige, damn it. He'd do it today. But not yet. The forest was calling too alluringly.

It was mid-morning, and the sun was striking through leaves still wet with melting frost. Sunbeams fractured. The forest floor crackled under foot. Birds flittered and chirruped. He knew the smell of the place, like he knew his own skin: new plants pushing up through old leaves; dead wood decaying; the damp richness of ferns and moss and lichen.

He wandered in gentle meanders,

circling the centre. He felt too pleasantly spaced out either to set out on a serious hike or to go back indoors and rest. Weeks of tension unspooled. He stretched his arms out wide, wide, and felt his lungs expand with good forest air.

And then he heard it. A noise he'd never heard in the forest before. A single animal, howling at the sky.

A wolf!

He had to be dreaming. There hadn't been wolves in the San Michele forest for five hundred years.

But then it came again and Jonas shook off his abstraction and snapped into action. There was something — or someone — real out there making that spine-chilling sound. Possibly hurt. One for Jonas, forest ranger!

He strode back into the centre and shouldered one of the rescue backpacks and went looking. He crossed and recrossed the trails systematically, as he'd been taught, but saw no animal tracks that could account for it.

Then he came to a clearing he recognized. And stopped dead. There was someone there. It was a secluded place. He'd never seen anyone here before except a fellow ranger. And she was no ranger. She was sitting on a fallen tree trunk, maybe twenty yards away. Turned away from him. Unaware.

The hand holding his hunter's knife fell to his side. Jonas drew a long breath.

She shimmered in the silvery spring sunshine. Hair a swirl of rainbows. Still as a dryad on a Greek frieze, yet somehow vibrantly alive. A creature of myth, at one with trees and the sparkling air.

Jonas shook his head hard and shut his eyes to clear his vision. But when he opened them, she was still there. Underneath those dancing rainbows, her hair was red. Her shoulders drooped. She was motionless.

Unnaturally so, he thought now, as his ranger awareness kicked into danger mode. Was she lost? Hurt? Was it her voice he'd heard, then? Not an animal at all, but a person? It had sounded so lonely. His heart turned over at the thought of a fellow human being so bereft.

He started forward, treading softly so as not to alarm her, but not trying to hide his approach either. She still didn't move. When he got within five yards of her, he stopped, as advised in the rangers' guidance on search and rescue. Panic, they always said, was the killer. You had to keep the subject calm, and that meant not creeping up behind them and spooking them.

He pitched his voice carefully, aiming for relaxed but reassuring. 'Hi there. Are you OK?'

The woman jumped and leaped off her tree trunk. She looked round wildly. So at least her limbs were all working, he thought. That was a good sign.

'I'm over here,' he said, not moving because you mustn't crowd a disoriented victim.

She pivoted, still searching. The

dappled shadow of the trees must be camouflaging him, because it took her a while. He took a small step forward and she found him at last. She looked wary. Or was it borderline alarmed?

Maybe she hadn't recognized the uniform. He said reassuringly, 'I'm a ranger.'

She frowned, seeming to concentrate hard, and eventually dredged up, 'I understand. No. *Not*. I *not* understand.'

So she was a visitor. Well, San Michele had more foreign residents than native-born citizens, though not many of them made it out this deep into the countryside.

He switched to English, the language of the city's most important economic activity. 'I'm a forest ranger. Do you need assistance, ma'am?' The last was pure Iowa State Uni, not San Michele forest rangers' style at all, but it seemed a good idea in the circumstances.

She understood him then. Their eyes met with a jolt. Jonas's head went back in shock. The redhead looked stunned.

And then a big dog-like animal moved out of the shadows into the sunlight, put back its head and howled like a soul in torment.

It *had* to be hurt. In pure instinct, Jonas flung himself forward, ready to wrestle the animal to the ground before it could attack her.

The woman's eyes widened. They stayed fixed on him. She backed away. She looked terrified.

'Stand very still,' he told her.

She stopped dead.

The dog looked at her, then him. Its lip curled back in a snarl. Jonas eased himself between the woman and the beast, no sharp movements, no haste.

'Back away now,' he said over his shoulder, maintaining eye contact with the animal. 'Calmly. Don't run.'

He could hear her agitated breathing. She was poised for flight. He knew it. But still she stayed rooted to the spot. Meanwhile the creature quivered, its hackles raised, jaws slavering.

Why didn't she *move*?

And then, to his astonishment, she spoke. Her voice was shaky but she said, 'It's all right, boy.'

Boy? Was she crazy?

He heard her swallow. Her voice strengthened. 'Good dog.'

The dog stayed where it was, eyeing Jonas. It looked ready to spring.

At last she was beginning to move. But not fleeing out of harm's way like he'd told her. Instead she was edging round the clearing in a wide arc. To his horror, she approached the dog from behind.

'Don't.' He held up his hand in the international halt signal.

But she kept creeping up until she was standing beside the dog. She even put her hand on the creature's head. Jonas felt his heart squeeze tight with dread.

But the dog didn't turn and attack. It accepted her hand, but it didn't make any other sign that it knew she was there. It watched Jonas, alert, quivering in every muscle. He thought it looked like a guard dog.

He said, 'Does this animal belong to you?'

At exactly the same second, she said, 'Will you please stop brandishing that machete? It worries him. And frankly, you're making me nervous.' The words were strong enough, but her voice was distinctly wobbly.

Jonas was taken aback. He glanced down at his hunting knife. It was sharp enough to cut back undergrowth and looked it. He supposed it was big if you weren't used to such things. He sheathed it carefully and looked up.

'Better?'

The woman nodded. She looked very pale.

In quick sympathy he said, 'Is the dog injured? Do you know?'

She stared. 'No. Why?'

'That howling to raise the dead.' Jonas was rueful. 'I thought it was wolves.'

'Wolves?' Her voice rose.

He'd obviously really scared her. And who could blame her? Strange man bursting out of the undergrowth waving a knife and telling her to run! How could he have been such an idiot?

He hastened to stop making bad worse. 'No, no. A mistake. No need to worry. Honestly. If a wolf showed up here today it would make the record books.'

She gave a little puff of relief and her shoulders came down. And then reaction set in. Anger. 'Then why think it?'

'Because it gave me a shock,' he said honestly. *And I'm running on empty after the week's work and last night. My judgement is shot.* But none of that was her fault. 'Look. Let's start again. This is your dog, right?'

She bristled visibly. 'And how is that your business?'

Jonas gestured to the badge on his all-weather jacket. 'I'm a forest ranger. Volunteer, here on a training programme. We have a code for dog walkers in the forest.'

'Oh.' That caught her on the wrong foot; but now that she had come out of panic mode, she was fighting her corner with a will. Her tone bit. 'Sorry, Moby made too much noise. But he isn't injured. He's sad.' She bent to rub the dog's head.

The creature butted her thigh in response, then flung itself on its back with its paws in the air and panted invitingly.

So not a wolf, thought Jonas. He was aware of an almost irresistible urge to laugh. 'Sad?' He couldn't quite keep the incredulity out of his voice.

She didn't laugh. Didn't even smile. Not even at the dog.

'His people have gone away on holiday. He misses them. I'm dog-sitting while they're away.'

'And you thought you'd bring him into the forest for a run?'

It wasn't an accusation, but she flushed and said defensively, 'The family do. They told me so. And the father is a lawyer and the permit is in the car. I checked.'

She looked adorable, unsure of her ground and hating it. The dappled sunlight was making those rainbows dance around her hair again, too. Jonas felt as if he had known her forever and understood her to her bones. Or was his judgement still off?

He wrestled his thoughts back into order. 'They probably didn't tell you we have a dog walking code?'

She winced.

'Don't worry. It's not complicated. Just good sense. But it's important to stick to the main paths at this time of year because we have ground-nesting birds. If a dog disturbs them, the birds can panic and leave their eggs.'

'*Oh!*' She looked mortified.

No otherworldly dryad now, he thought. This was a wholly twenty-first century woman in jeans and a utilitarian fleece. She had mud on those jeans and twigs caught up in her wild red hair.

He wanted to gather her up in his

arms, smooth the worry lines from her forehead and tell her there was no harm done yet.

Get a grip. That's completely out of order, and you know it. Well, you do when you're in your right mind.

'Look,' he said, 'it's no big deal. You'll be fine, now that you know. I can give you another copy of the forest code for dog walkers if you drop by the rangers' centre. You and Moby are very welcome to San Michele forest.' And he held out his hand.

She didn't seem to notice it. 'Really?'

He let his hand fall but he was not deterred. 'Really. Just learn a bit about the lie of the land before you start playing in the trees with Moby. You're a long way off any of the regular paths here, you know. In fact, are you sure you can find your way back to your vehicle?'

She stiffened. 'I did make notes of the way we came. I didn't think about birds, I admit, but I did do that.'

He'd heard that from other footsore

walkers whom the rangers had turned out to rescue and return home. He didn't say so. Instead he asked, 'OK. Where did you leave your car?'

She described the place as best she could. Jonas didn't ask questions or prompt her in any way, and he saw her slowly realize that she had no real idea of where she'd left the car at all. She fell silent mid-sentence.

When he was certain she wasn't going to say any more, he said carefully, 'I think I know the place. I can guide you back there, if you like.'

Even aware that she might be lost in the forest, she wasn't giving an inch. She shook her head. 'I couldn't ask you to do that.'

Aha, thought Jonas, who had qualified as a lawyer in London. 'British, right?'

'What?'

'*I couldn't ask you to do that* is British English for sod off.'

She stiffened. 'It's English for I couldn't ask you to do that.'

'But you're not asking. I'm offering,' he pointed out, amused.

'You have your own stuff to do,' she said between her teeth.

Jonas was beginning to enjoy himself. 'This *is* my own stuff. Rescuing people lost in the forest is what rangers do.'

For a moment he thought she would scream with frustration. He waited hopefully.

But she regrouped well. After a moment she said with icy dignity, 'Thank you, but I've got my notes. I just have to trust them.'

'And the odds are that you'll get lost again. Then one or more of us will have to come out looking for you.'

'I wouldn't ask — '

'I'm sure you wouldn't. But I have to report that I've seen you; and then, if you don't come out of the forest in a couple of hours, we'd have to set up a search and rescue operation.'

She didn't like that. 'How would you know that I hadn't come out of the forest?'

'If your car was still where you left it. *I* know where it is.' He didn't have to add, *Unlike you*.

She went down fighting. 'Moby can probably find the way.'

Jonas just looked at the dog, still wriggling on the fallen leaves with paws flying and eyes closed in ecstasy. Even the spiky dryad seemed to take the point. She gave a snort, quickly cut off, but he thought there was just a faint possibility that she was starting to see the funny side of this encounter, too.

Encouraged, he said, 'Look, if I'm right, your car is maybe ten minutes from here.'

That startled her, he saw. She must have been walking in a wide circle from the Crossways Clearing.

'Ten minutes,' he said persuasively. 'Then, if you really want to be helpful, you can drive me back to the rangers' centre.'

He watched with appreciation as deep dudgeon warred with British courtesy. In the end, courtesy won. But it cost her. Interesting. Did she hate having been in the wrong that much? Or was there something else going on here?

'Very well,' she said stiffly.

'Thank you.'

She nodded, called the dog, and went with Jonas. He led the way back. She wasn't obvious about it, but he noticed that she made sure the dog was between them at all times. It needled him, but he took himself to task. It was a sensible precaution for a lone woman in an unfamiliar place to take with any stranger, even one in a ranger's uniform. She was obviously used to taking care of herself. Maybe she hadn't needed his assistance, after all.

But when they got back to her car, she stopped dead and looked around. 'I set off from over there,' she said in a wondering voice. She pointed to a small animal track on the other side of the clearing. 'How did I manage to get here?'

'If you come into the centre, I'll show

you on the big map,' Jonas said, tempting her.

She looked at him for a long moment. He couldn't read her expression, but he felt the tension shift. He waited for her to make up her mind.

She said slowly, 'I've been making a complete prat of myself, haven't I?'

Jonas shrugged. 'You're quite safe with me. But then I'd say that anyway, wouldn't I?'

'Yes.'

He nodded, accepting her tacit decision. 'Well, I'm glad you and Moby have found your vehicle, at least. Take my advice. Don't go wandering in the forest again without a map of the trails. And get a copy of the code. It's not just ground-nesting birds. There are wild pigs and even cattle in some places. You need to be prepared. You can download everything from our website, if you don't want to pick one up at the centre.' He turned away. 'Safe journey.'

But she surprised him. 'Wait!'

Jonas turned back. Their eyes locked.

Her gaze flickered, became intent. He straightened involuntarily. Suddenly his pulse was racing.

'Thank you for rescuing me,' she said gruffly. 'I mean us, Moby and me.'

Well, that was unexpected. He brought his voice under control and tipped an imaginary hat. 'Code of the rangers, ma'am.'

Her eyes lit with instant grateful amusement and she smiled at him for the first time. It took his breath away. Was it his irregular pulse, or were they remarkable eyes? Clear. Candid. Warm hazel with flickers of witch green. Was that even possible? Eyes that seemed to look right through to the core of him. Jonas felt as if he was smiling right back into her as if they were already . . .

. . . already . . .

Friends?

Yes. And?

Allies. Each other's confidant. Companions in forest exploration.

Oh, come on, Jonas. Witch-green eyes and you just want to go hiking with her? Get real.

Lovers, then. The moment the word occurred to him, it seemed to whisper through his whole being, mind, blood and bone. Right. Inevitable.

He came back, with an effort, to what she was saying.

'I'm truly sorry. We were lucky you came along.'

'You're welcome.'

She laughed aloud at that. 'Very generous, and more than I deserve. I promise I'll take your advice from now on.'

Jonas seized his chance. He patted the side of the 4×4 as if it were a horse. 'Back to the centre then?'

She shook back her tumble of red curls and their attendant rainbows and laughed again. 'Whatever you say, ranger.'

He found he couldn't speak.

So this time it was she who held out her hand. 'I'm Hope Kennard. New to San Michele, the forest, and apologies. Glad to have made all three. Good to meet you.'

He took her hand. It was cool and

firm. The blood in his fingertips tingled as if he'd touched a live electric connection. 'Jonas,' he said, distracted.

She shook his hand firmly. 'Jonas what?'

He hesitated for a millisecond. But her eyes were dancing now, and she'd called him ranger. There were no Serene Highnesses in the forest. So the die was already cast.

'Jonas Reval,' he said firmly.

3

Hope couldn't help it. She thought, *He's lying.* And was instantly ashamed of herself.

The man had been nothing but kind. Tried to protect her from a wolf, and then brought her back to find her car, instead of leaving her to get on with it, which would have taken hours. He hadn't taken offence when she ranted at him. He'd got her back to the clearing in just a few minutes without saying, 'I told you so.' That would earn him high marks in anybody's book. He'd been tolerant, helpful and funny. He deserved better than groundless suspicion.

Except that it wasn't — quite — groundless. Hope knew how people behaved when they were lying. Her father had done it all the time.

But Jonas Reval was nothing like her father, she told herself now. Maybe the ranger was a bit too sexy for his own good. Even over the uneven forest floor he moved beautifully, as if his joints were oiled and he couldn't wait to break into a run, just for the pleasure of springing from foot to foot. But it was hardly his fault that she was attracted to lithe men. He'd showed no sign of noticing her reaction, anyway. And just now he had even made her laugh.

If she mistrusted him, it was all in her own head. She was letting her old wariness get out of hand. It was about time she got over it.

So she waved the ranger to get into the vehicle, while Moby scrambled into the back. When she swung into the driving seat, their shoulders touched and she jumped. *Stop it*, she told herself silently. Aloud she said, 'You'll need to navigate.'

'Of course.' He gave her directions. And Hope, who had driven everything from a stretch limousine to stock cars in mud, crashed the gears for the first time in her life.

She found it strangely awkward driving the ranger back to his centre. He gave her a prickly, restless feeling. She felt as if he never took his eyes off her. Yet when she managed to glance casually sideways, he was leaning forward checking the track ahead, not looking at her at all.

'Ah, thought so. Big pothole here,' he said helpfully.

Hope wrenched the vehicle round it just in time. Even so, they bumped hard, and poor Moby in the back gave a hiccupping bark of protest.

Jonas laughed. 'Back-seat driver,' he said, and reached behind to let the dog sniff his hand. But he kept his eyes on the rough terrain ahead, Hope saw.

Eventually he directed her off the vestigial track. At his direction, she threaded her way between substantial trees. The off-roader lurched sickeningly a couple of times. But Hope gritted her teeth and kept it steady. He seemed impressed.

'You've done this before?'

'I was brought up in the country. I was driving through my family's woods before I was old enough to get a driving licence.'

'It shows,' he said approvingly. 'One last heave over the next rise and we're onto the main track again.'

The nose lifted like the prow of a boat in a rough sea, but Hope was prepared for it this time. 'Thar she blows,' she crowed as they breasted the summit with a bone-shaking thump. Concentrating, she turned the steering wheel gently so that they descended the far side at an optimal trajectory to the rate of decline.

'Very cool.'

She was just bouncing off the forest floor and onto a visibly beaten track when he said that, so she didn't have any spare attention to reply. But she had the impression that she had surprised him. It was comforting after all that amateur gear-crashing she'd done when they started.

The rangers' centre proved to be a

huddle of single-storey buildings that looked as if it had grown organically, rather than been designed and constructed by hand. Hope said so, then wondered too late if he would count it as an insult.

But he just laughed and said, 'About right. It started off as a woodman's cottage a couple of hundred years ago. Bits got added. Now it's part rangers' HQ, part education centre. Come and see.'

He jumped down from the vehicle and went in. Hope paused to put Moby on his lead before she followed more slowly. Inside were two men, one white-haired holding a massive walking stick, and one middle-aged, both watching Jonas write on a whiteboard. There was also a delicious smell of coffee. Hope stopped dead, her nose twitching with lust.

Jonas turned and saw her expression. 'Ah. You'd like a coffee. Guys, this is Hope Kennard, with Moby, who is not a wolf.'

The other two hooted. 'Better luck next time, young Jonas,' said the middle-aged one.

'Miss Hope looks better than a wolf to me,' said the one with the stick, beaming. 'Well done, lad.'

Jonas and the other man rolled their eyes.

'Thank you, Marko,' said Jonas dryly. 'Hope, may I introduce Klaus, the bringer of coffee. He's also ranger supremo. Cro-Magnon man over there is Marko.'

Hope laughed. 'I'm flattered,' she assured Marko, and accepted coffee from Klaus. It was black, steaming, and smelled gorgeous. She closed her eyes and absorbed it, revelling 'Mmm.'

There was an odd little silence. She opened her eyes but the other two weren't looking at her. Their eyes were on Jonas. He looked as if he'd been stuffed.

'I mean, thank you,' she said hurriedly, conscious of a shortfall in manners.

Jonas cleared his throat. 'You're welcome. I'll — er — just go and get rid of my stuff. Klaus, why don't you show Hope on the map where she's been? I found her just short of the lower birch grove. She'd left her vehicle at Cross-ways Clearing. Oh, and she needs a dog walkers' code.'

It seemed to Hope that he bolted like a rabbit down a burrow. She raised her eyebrows.

'There'll be clean socks in his room,' explained Cro-Magnon man comfort-ably. 'Lot of mud between here and the lower birch grove.'

'His room?' Hope was astonished. 'He lives here?'

The other two looked at each other. 'What did he tell you?'

'Just that he's a ranger. A volunteer ranger. So that would make him pretty much bottom of the food chain, I assume?'

Klaus gave a crack of laughter, which he turned into a cough. But Marko nodded. 'About right,' he said with satisfaction. 'Boy's got a lot to learn.'

Hope found a contrary desire to stand up for Jonas, in spite of his high-handed ways. 'He had enough experience to lead me out of the forest when I got lost,' she pointed out.

Marko opened his mouth but Klaus interrupted quickly. 'Jonas is very experienced in the forest. You couldn't have been in better hands,' he said, frowning Marko down. 'He's a regular volunteer, and he's even done a degree in wilderness studies in America.'

Marko snorted. He clearly didn't think much of wilderness studies.

'So do all of your volunteers have a room here?'

'Good point. No. But Jonas has just arrived for a fortnight of full-time volunteering. We always try to get people up here in the spring. That's when we get high winds, floods sometimes, even a fire when it's been a dry winter like now.'

And he launched happily into a description of the rangers' duties and organization. Then he remembered to show her the map and trace the course she must have taken. He gave her three leaflets, one with a history of the forest and a map on the back, the dog walkers' code, and one on safety. Hope skimmed the latter, wincing. She'd broken every one of the first three forest etiquette protocols already. She folded it and put it carefully in her pocket.

'I'll go through this properly when I get home. I've clearly got a lot to learn.'

'Jonas can help you with that,' suggested Marko. 'Next two weeks, you'll find him here, day and night.'

Klaus looked exasperated. 'Except when he's out on patrol or doing some element of his refresher course.'

'Then Miss Hope had better try night-time then, hadn't she? He won't be out on patrol then. Not unless there's an emergency.'

Klaus breathed hard. 'As I've just been explaining, spring is the time when there are emergencies. And Jonas is here to work, not socialize.'

Marko waved that aside. 'If you're thinking of that professor person, she won't be back until the summer. And anyway, she's over sixty. Fine-looking woman, mind,' he added, momentarily sidetracked from Jonas.

Klaus snorted and muttered something in his own language that Hope had no difficulty at all in interpreting as a variant of *randy old goat*. She had the greatest difficulty in keeping a straight face. 'I see that the rangers are a close-knit bunch, volunteers or not.'

'We look out for each other,' said Klaus with emphasis.

Marko ignored his hard stare and agreed blithely. 'Yes, even when they live in Liburno, like young Jonas. Of course, he can't help it.' The stare became positively ferocious.

'Really?' said Hope, quite looking forward to a further joust. Clearly Klaus was hopping mad and, even more clearly, Marko enjoyed winding him up.

Now Marko grinned at the senior

ranger and said, 'Being as he's a lawyer. Don't know how long you've been here, Miss Hope. But if you don't know yet, you'll soon find out. Liburno is lawyer central. Can't throw a brick in the centre of town without hitting one.'

Klaus's glare could have made a fair-sized bonfire burst into flames. Hope judged that it was time to negotiate a truce.

'That's very interesting. I'm ashamed to say all I know about San Michele is in the preface to my phrasebook.'

'Then Jonas is definitely the man to tell you all about it,' said Marko with a chuckle.

'All about what?' Jonas appeared in the doorway. He'd rid himself of the backpack and lost the wet-weather gear and heavy boots. Without them, he looked taller and somehow more muscular, thought Hope. Sort of at ease in his skin and calm, as if he could handle anything and knew it.

That was when he noticed her looking at him. And looked back. Hope went very still. Hot, she thought, suddenly confused. Very hot.

Marko was saying something. She had no idea what. Jonas looked amused. Oh dear Lord. When he was amused, his eyes sparkled as if he expected her to share the joke. Hotter and hotter.

Moby, who'd been sprawled peacefully by the desk with his nose on his paws, suddenly sat up, pulling on his chain.

Hope came to herself with a jump. 'Time I was going,' she said over the residual ringing in her ears. 'Thank you for coffee and forest guidance. I'll do better next time. Goodbye.'

'I'll walk you out,' said Jonas serenely.

To her dismay, she dissolved into what she'd have called flustered spinster mode in anyone else. 'Um — no need but — um — thank you and — er — Moby's dinner time. Goodbye.' She fled.

Jonas got to the door before her and

held it open courteously. Moby managed to tangle himself round her legs, so that she went first one way, then the other, and ended nearly falling over him. All the while Jonas stood there holding the door, with a look of unholy appreciation.

Hope made Moby stand still while she stepped over the entangling dog lead. Then she grabbed him firmly by the collar and scooted him towards the car. 'I am not a flustered spinster,' she muttered.

'Excuse me?' said blasted Jonas, too close behind her.

Hope tripped over her own feet and nearly fell. Moby stopped and looked at her with well-earned reproach.

'May I?' Without waiting for a reply, Jonas possessed himself of Moby's lead, gave the dog a reassuring head rub, hoisted him into the back of the vehicle, lead and all, and firmly closed the door on him.

Meanwhile Hope fought for composure. 'Thank you,' she said with a dignified gratitude she was rather proud of. It was completely phoney.

Jonas knew it, too. His eyes sparkled. 'You're very welcome.'

She could well believe it. She got behind the driving wheel, but before she could close the door on him, he was beside her, all courteous anxiety. She ground her teeth and managed a gracious nod. It did not have the desired effect. He still stood there, door open.

'Will you be all right?'

When I get my mind back. 'In what way?' she asked suspiciously.

His mouth stayed grave. How could he do that when his eyes laughed like demons?

'I mean, will you be able to find your way home?'

'Yes,' Hope said recklessly. She didn't care if she had to go home via the mountains or even across an international border. Somewhere on the road she would find a stranger to give her directions. Anybody would do. Anything was better than Jonas Reval as in-car navigator.

She reached out with determination and closed the driver's door. 'Goodbye.'

'I'll be in touch.'

He'd brought out a smart phone and was standing there, waiting for her to give him her number, Hope saw. Once again, she had that tiny flicker of mistrust. He was too confident, somehow. The last time she'd ignored her instincts had not turned out so well, she reminded herself.

'No need,' she said with a pleasant smile. Yes, that was the right tone, friendly but firm.

It didn't have the desired effect. 'Not at all. It will be my pleasure.'

Mistrust was swamped by sheer outrage. She was not going to be railroaded into doing something she didn't feel comfortable with, just because a man was charming and looked sexy in a ranger's uniform. She said to herself as much as him, 'Look, I'm fine. And so is Moby. Neither of us needs babysitting.'

'That's excellent news.' He was bland. 'Then we can leave him home when I take you out for the evening.'

Hope closed her eyes and counted to ten. Then she opened them and said with a calm as great as his own, 'Good try but no sale, Mr Reval.'

And for some reason that did the trick. He looked stricken. She had no idea why, but that didn't matter; she was just grateful for the chance to get away. Hope had learned much on her travels, and seizing the moment came right at the top of the list.

Now was the moment. She gave him a friendly wave and drove off.

4

The relief wore off, of course. By the time they got home, Hope was kicking herself for being too suspicious.

OK, the last job had ended in a mess because she'd ignored her instincts and allowed herself to be manoeuvred into being nice to someone she didn't really like. Then her employer's friend had interpreted her friendly courtesy as something very different, and he hadn't taken his rejection well. In fact, that was the real reason that she'd left.

But she *did* like Jonas Reval. So why was she being so wary?

I had that feeling he wasn't being straight with me.

Yes, but she had no reason for it. They'd hardly got up close and personal yet. She could at least have given him a chance.

Against my instincts?

There was no right answer.

That didn't stop thoughts of Jonas Reval going round and round in her head over the following days. It was as if he had spun a web round her, she thought.

'Are you OK?' asked Poppy the third day after their forest encounter. And before Hope could answer she said, 'I'm not. Mother's trying to make me go to a party.'

She sounded so woebegone that Hope had to laugh. But she sympathized too. 'Really bad party?'

Poppy nodded vigorously. 'The worst. Huge party. Two girls from school. And I have to have a new dress.'

'Well, that could be fun, couldn't it?'

Poppy curled her upper lip back from the heavy brace. 'Teeth stay the same.'

'Ouch,' said Hope, instantly comprehending.

'Could you possibly tell Mother that Moby has gone off his food and I absolutely must come home and take care of him or he'll die?'

'I don't think she'd believe me.'

That clearly hadn't occurred to Poppy. 'You could at least tell her you wouldn't mind babysitting me as well as Moby, if I came home.'

'With pleasure,' said Hope, thinking that Poppy's company would be a great distraction from worrying away at the problem of whether she should go back to the rangers' centre and whether Jonas Reval would be there if she did. And what message that would give him if he was.

But Poppy's mother, when Hope spoke to her, had other issues on her mind. 'Can you go into town and pick up our post, do you think?' she said distractedly. 'We're supposed to be getting an invitation to the vintage ball, and my husband's office says it's been sent to the villa.'

'I'll give it my best shot. I'll need some authority.' Hope was good at forecasting bureaucracy and worked out a rapid list.

'You're brilliant,' said her grateful

employer. 'I'd never thought of all that.'

'No problem. And by the way, Poppy asked me to tell you it was fine with me if you wanted to send her home. I'd be happy to babysit her as well as Moby. No extra charge.'

Her employer sighed. 'This is Poppy trying to get out of the yacht club spring bash, right? I just don't understand her. I'd have killed for the chance to go to a grown-up party at her age.'

Hope saw her opportunity. 'Um — did you wear braces on your teeth?'

But all Mrs Anton said was, 'Let me know when you've got the post, would you?'

So Hope took a briefcase full of enough official-looking paper to gladden any bureaucrat's heart, and drove into town. The post office was next door to the station, high-ceilinged, with a handsome marble counter, adorned with a full set of Edwardian brasswork and almost empty except for an elderly woman in a headscarf — and a man in a ranger's all-weather jacket.

Hope's heart lurched. *Jonas!* She stopped dead so that poor Moby skidded on the marble tiles and yelped. It couldn't be!

It was. He was talking to a man in an impressive-looking uniform, whom Hope judged to be the postmaster. It looked like a disagreement, but for once the bureaucrat seemed to be the one who was pleading. Hope smiled at that and, equilibrium restored, went forward.

'Good morning,' she said breezily.

Jonas spun round, made a noise remarkably like Moby's, and dropped a sheaf of papers as substantial as her own. They shot across the marble like ball bearings on ice. The woman in the headscarf flung herself after them, clucking and twittering as she gathered them up.

'*You!*' he said. He looked genuinely shocked.

'Nice to see you again too.'

'I didn't — I was just saying — ' He broke off, looking harassed, as the headscarfed woman pressed his retrieved papers into his hand, nodding and smiling and damn near curtseying. He smiled and shook her hand, then said something rapid to the postmaster. The woman backed away, bobbing and smiling. The postmaster bowed and started to retreat as well.

'Hey,' Hope called after him, 'don't go. I need to collect some post.'

But the postmaster seemed tongue-tied. He looked wildly at Jonas.

'Sorry. I thought everyone spoke English,' said Hope with a friendly smile. She fished her phrasebook out of her shoulderbag and began to flick through it.

Jonas said something in his own language and the postmaster stepped forward, straightening his jacket. 'How can I help you, miss?'

She explained her errand and prepared to break out her supply of signed instructions, proofs of identity and assorted passwords and other codes, but it all seemed too much for the postmaster. He looked at Jonas, who gave an almost imperceptible nod.

'There is no need for formality,' said

the postmaster. 'Since you have a — er — resident to vouch for you. And you are also accompanied by Mr Anton's dog, I see. I shall attend to the matter at once.' He departed in a stately way, leaving Hope standing with her folder of unwanted documents, feeling foolish.

'I thought it would be more bureaucratic than that.'

Jonas was smiling into her eyes as if they were old friends. More than friends. 'It's a small town. Everyone knows everybody else's business.'

Hope felt breathless. Suddenly the world was full of sunshine, in spite of the scudding clouds outside. She said something; she didn't know what.

'You haven't been back to the forest?'

She managed not to blush and said vaguely, 'Busy. You know how it is.'

'Oh, I do.' He looked at his watch. 'Look, do you have to be somewhere? Or have you time for a coffee?'

Which nicely got rid of the need to decide whether to go to the rangers' centre. 'I think I could manage that.'

He gave a sigh of relief. 'Great.'

The postmaster returned with a canvas bag of post and a leather-bound embossed register. He ceremonially completed the details, took note of the number of her passport and, with a minatory look at Jonas, pointedly asked her to sign that she had received the Anton family's post.

Jonas hoisted the bag over his shoulder as Hope thanked the postmaster and shook hands with him.

Hope was curious about that odd look. 'What was that about?'

Jonas didn't pretend to misunderstand. 'I was asking if he'd met you. Knew where you lived. But he started quoting clauses of the Post Office Act and talking about confidentiality.'

She was taken aback. 'Sounds a bit extreme!'

He nodded, rueful. 'I was on the point of calling him a drama queen when you arrived. So thank you for saving me from that.'

He took her to a pretty café with lace

curtains and a delicious smell of coffee.

'Ah,' said Hope, stopping in the doorway to inhale luxuriously.

'Yes, I thought you would go for that,' he said, watching her with amusement. He identified a table and snapped his fingers at Moby, who slid underneath and tucked in his paws and tail as if he were born to undercover surveillance.

'He's done that before,' they both said in unison, and their eyes met as they laughed.

The laughter died away, but their eyes stayed locked. A fatherly waiter came over and Jonas ordered in his own language, without asking Hope what she wanted. She barely noticed. He seemed to be saying everything important with his eyes. She hadn't a clue what it meant, but it made her feel as if her blood were fizzing and she could dance on the table and burst into song if she wanted.

I've never felt like this before. What's happening to me?

Somebody ought to say something. The café wasn't busy, but if they just sat and stared at each other like this, people would start to notice. She said at random, 'I thought you were on a course with the rangers. What are you doing in town?'

'Looking for you.'

'What?'

'Well, I'd drawn a blank everywhere else,' he said, injured. 'You'd said you were working for a lawyer, but you didn't give us a *name*. None of the rangers recognized your vehicle or even Moby. And social media was a wash-out.'

That gave her a nasty jolt. The creepy employer's friend had uncovered her family scandal and tried to use it to make her, as he put it, grateful. That was what had precipitated the final showdown. She winced. 'Did you google me?'

'Yes. Nothing useful. You're a woman of mystery. I couldn't find so much as a discontinued Facebook page.'

Well, he wouldn't. When her father was first arrested, there had been a deluge of abuse against all the family. In particular, the Facebook page of fourteen-year-old Hope at an exclusive boarding school had been irresistible to the crazier sorts of trolls. Hope had closed down all her social media outlets within a month of the news getting into the papers.

She had to ask, 'Did you look just for me? Nobody else?'

'I don't know anyone else to look for.'

'Not my family?'

He shrugged. 'I admit that eventually I took a gamble and added British. That netted me a few possible sightings, all on other people's blogs. One in the French Alps last year. Another in Queensland, Australia, the year before. Were they you?'

It wasn't a complete answer. Was he being deliberately evasive? She pretended to consider, while she weighed her options. 'Sounds about right.'

To tell him or not to tell him? Tell Jonas her late father was a convicted fraudster and watch him withdraw? Or let the fantasy run a little longer? Just while they had coffee and he looked at her as if she were the only woman in the world. Just *once*.

'You ran a ski chalet in France? And a flying school in Oz?'

Was once too much to ask?

'I didn't *run* the flying school. Just the office.'

'That's not how the blog described it,' he said dryly. 'But that's not the point. Why the different jobs? And the country-hopping?'

Hope took refuge in flippancy. 'I like variety.'

'And you never go back,' he said.

Ah. Mrs Brass from the chalet group must have put that on her blog after Hope left. And heaven knew what else. There was no point in trying to keep secrets. It had left her vulnerable when the creep at the chalet had made his move on her. Anyway, if Jonas was interested, he'd find out sooner or later. Why not get it over with now?

They were interrupted by the waiter bringing coffee and a dish of almond biscuits. A turbulence under the table indicated that Moby had sniffed out the cookies. Jonas laughed and slid one down to the dog.

It felt so sweet and normal, somehow. Hope made a decision. She always told the truth when asked, anyway. This time she didn't want to wait.

She cradled her coffee cup, trying to think of a way to introduce the subject. Jonas waited, relaxed but watchful. Eventually she said, 'You know British English, right? The idioms, I mean.'

He looked blank. 'I suppose so.'

'Have you heard the term a *guest of Her Majesty*?'

He tensed. 'Don't think so. Why?'

Her mouth was very dry. She took a sip of coffee. It was too hot. She pushed it away. She didn't look at him. 'It means being in prison.'

He didn't ask why, again. Just sat

very still, listening.

She looked at her hands on the pretty tablecloth. They were competent, neat-fingered and strong. She liked her hands. 'When I was growing up, my father went to prison.'

He said slowly, 'He's still there?'

She shook her head. 'He died in prison before I started travelling. Kidney disease. He'd never been strong.' For no reason she could think of, she added, 'It wasn't the prison's fault. They were quite kind to him, I think. He said so, anyway.'

'Does that help?' It was very gentle.

She looked up then, searching his face. Jonas looked concerned, but he didn't seem shocked. She blinked rapidly. 'Do you know, no one's ever asked me that before. Yes, maybe it does.'

'You visited him? They let children visit prisons in Britain?'

'I was a teenager, not a kid. And yes, if you follow procedure. I'm good with procedures now.' She ticked it off on her fingers. 'Organize a date with an accompanying adult. Book in. Take my passport along for the security checks. And a pound coin to put my belongings in a locker. You're not allowed to take anything with you when you see the prisoner. It's a bit of a faff, but it's not rocket science.'

'Oh, sweetheart.' He reached across the table to take her hands.

Hope hadn't expected it and shied away. 'Don't be kind to me. I just wanted you to know. From me.'

His arm fell to his side. Eventually he said, 'So you started travelling when he died?'

That was much easier to talk about. She smiled, remembering. 'No, not immediately. I'd made a deal with my brother. If he'd be my required adult when I went to visit the prison, I'd finish school. So I did.'

'You keep your promises.' It seemed to please him.

'Oh yes. It's bad luck not to. I've got a real hang-up about it.' Her father had never understood about keeping promises, poor lamb. He'd faced up to what he'd done, in the end, but he'd never been able to grasp why it was so wrong.

'Was it hard?'

She thought about it. 'I don't know,' she said honestly. 'You do what you have to when there's no alternative. It was tougher for my brother than me, I think. His marriage broke up. Of course, my mother was long gone by then.'

Jonas sat bolt upright at that. 'What?'

Hope was rueful but resigned. She'd had a long time to come to terms with it, after all. Now she pulled a face. 'Mama took off as soon as Dad was arrested. She had friends who gathered her up and took her off on lots of holidays. She left my brother and me to get on with it.'

Jonas looked affronted. 'You're joking.'

Hope was surprised, because this was something that had never really hurt her. 'Max was grown up and married.'

'What on earth did the woman think she was doing?' He sounded furious.

'Doubt if she thought much at all,' said Hope dispassionately. 'I was pretty much an adult by then anyway.'

'Hell's teeth, Hope!'

'Look, I liked my mother but we were never close, even before the crash. I was always getting muddy and driving tractors, while she was a real girly girl. When my father fell by the wayside, she just found someone else, that's all. Nobody was surprised.'

Jonas blinked. 'Phew! If that's what you say about someone you like, heaven help me if you take against me.'

Hope laughed then, really laughed. 'My mother would have said the same herself. She was quite honest about it.'

Jonas shook his head, disbelieving.

'You'd have liked her,' said Hope, entertained. 'She was very charming.'

'Was?'

Hope sobered. 'Yes. That was a bad shock. She died two years after Dad. Dived off a yacht one night after a party and hit her head.'

'That must have been tough.'

'Ye-es. Up to a point.' The truth was more complicated than that. She eyed him speculatively. Would he be shocked by how she and Max had reacted? She took a gamble and said, 'Max said it must have been a helluva party.'

There was stunned silence. Then he threw back his head and laughed.

Hope smiled brilliantly, relieved and a little shy. 'We decided to be glad that she died when she was having fun. We raise a glass of champagne to her whenever we get together.'

Jonas stopped laughing. 'That sounds good,' he said slowly. 'Really good. My mother died when I was small. I don't know if she ever had any fun.' It sounded bleak. As if he heard it himself and needed to banish the feelings he'd brought up, he leaned forward, suddenly alert. 'Look, why don't *we* have some fun? Spend the rest of the day together?'

Hope could feel her smile stretching from ear to ear. 'Kick up our heels? That's what my mother used to call it.'

'Kick up our heels,' he agreed. 'And I know just the way to do it.'

* * *

It was the start of a wholly new experience. Jonas had never thought so much about a woman, nor worked so hard at a relationship in his life.

Certainly not with the well-connected young ladies Anna kept trawling in front of him. Nor with any of the girlfriends he'd had in England. Even in the States, where he'd hung out with the fans of his roommate's band and learned to dance the night away with experts, he'd never set out to plan a major exercise in fun.

It was great. Partly, he admitted to himself, that was a purely masculine relish of the challenge. But partly, it was because of the way Hope threw herself into things. She hadn't lied when she said she liked variety. She scrambled up a steep slope, under the spray of a waterfall that was fed to torrent-power by melting mountain snow, and just laughed when it knocked her off her feet and drenched her. She clawed her way up the wall-mounted iron ladder inside the disused fire tower like a bandy-legged monkey and swore the view from the top was worth every bruise and scrape.

Above all, he persuaded her to come with him on his routine forest patrols, much to the amusement of his fellow rangers. She brought Moby, whose exuberance in jumping in last year's leaves made them both laugh. But most important of all, she had such genuine curiosity about all the familiar plants and creatures and landscape that he felt he was seeing them afresh.

He noticed that she never mentioned her family again and she never asked him one thing about his own. So he followed her lead. They would live wholly in the present until she changed her mind.

So the present had better last as long as he could make it. He called his brother the crown prince, now returned from his business trip. As senior partner, Carlo was technically Jonas's boss.

'Hi, Jonas,' said Carlo cheerily. 'Having a good time? Working hard?' He knew that the main object of the holiday was the rangers' refresher course.

Jonas laughed. 'Holiday is more like it. We only work in the mornings and this week it's all about search and rescue. So another guy and I roam round the forest with the instructor, flexing our muscles and being Tarzan.'

'Sounds exciting,' said Carlo, just a touch wistfully, Jonas thought.

'You should try it. But look, Carlo, there's a lot of stuff to do, too, and I could do with some extra leave.'

Carlo hesitated audibly.

'A week? Maybe ten days?' said Jonas, trying not to sound too urgent. When Carlo still said nothing, he saw he would have to come clean. 'There's this woman. She's . . . different.'

There was another silence from Carlo. 'Tell.'

Jonas sighed. 'Nothing to tell. That's

why I need more time.'

'I see.' Carlo was uncomfortable. 'I know Anna's been pushing eligible women at you. This isn't some kind of statement, is it? An 'I'll have a fling if I want to' sort of thing?'

Jonas was shocked that his brother could think that. 'Of course not.'

'So it's serious?'

Oh yes, it was serious all right. On his side. 'Early days. You know how it is.'

'I'm not sure I do.' Carlo sounded sad.

Jonas said gently, 'That's why I need more time to be with her. See if she might feel the same.'

'Ah. Yes, of course.' Jonas could almost see his brother pulling himself together. 'Well, I don't see why not. You'd cleared your desk beautifully, I hear. Is anything likely to blow up with any of your clients?'

'If it does, call me and I'll sort it.'

'In that case, take as long as you want,' said Carlo, and rang off.

Jonas was grateful. He did all the

refresher stuff conscientiously, but his day didn't really start until Hope arrived. He was beginning to think she felt the same. And her delight in the forest just bubbled out of her.

'I'm so happy,' she said one day just as he looked up at the sky and raised his binoculars to a distant speck. 'Oh, what is it?'

'It could be a golden eagle.' He tried to refocus the binoculars. 'I'm not sure. I can't see the shape of its wings properly. The light's not right and it's too far without a proper 'scope. It could just be a buzzard.'

She chuckled. 'You make the poor buzzard sound like a second-class citizen.'

Jonas lowered the binoculars. 'I do, don't I? And he's an impressive chap, too. But the eagle is half as big again. More important, they're rare. They were nearly wiped out by hunting and DDT. Their numbers are only just beginning to recover.'

'So it's one for the whiteboard.'

He had pulled out the notebook from his inner pocket and was making a note of place, date and time of the sighting; but at this he looked up, enchanted. 'We'll make a ranger of you yet.'

'Sous ranger, maybe.'

'Huh?'

'Like sous chef. Junior assistant to fetch, carry and learn.'

That didn't sound good. 'Ouch. You're saying I'm exploiting you.'

But she shook her head, the witch-green eyes gleaming. 'Fetching and carrying are fine. And learning is a privilege. You're a good teacher. Carry on, Batman. With you every step of the way.'

He wanted to hug her. But a major part of the grand plan was not to touch her until she wanted him to. And so far she had shown no sign of it. Jonas might be new to these feelings, but he'd flirted with the best and he could see that little distance she kept between them as if it had been bright green sea glass.

Don't rush her. There's no hurry. Take it at her pace. It was an effort, but he managed to remind himself in time.

He finished writing and put the notebook back in his pocket. 'You're right. Definitely one for the whiteboard. We haven't sighted an eagle for a couple of years.'

Hope was intrigued. So he took his mind off wanting to hug her by launching into a lecture about how the bird had been hunted in the nineteenth century and poisoned by assorted agricultural practices in the twentieth.

'All the countries of the region got together and we banned hunting eagles across the whole area. Now no one who has shot an eagle can duck over a national border and feel safe, not once we know who he is. And even better than that, we've made it an offence to disturb the eagles' habitat. Of course, the wind farm lobby want to overturn that now. And so the battle goes on.'

'You enjoy it,' she said on a note of discovery.

He thought about it. 'No, it's not that exactly. I don't like fighting. It never gets you anywhere. If you lose, you feel resentful and carry on being as awkward as you can. And if you win, everyone hates you and won't let you win again. What I like is finding ways through the issues, so that everyone gets something.'

'So why are you a lawyer, instead of protecting the eagles full-time?'

He made a face. 'Long story.'

At once she stiffened. 'Oh. Sorry. I didn't mean to be nosy.'

Hell! He hadn't seen that coming. And now she'd retreated even further behind that sea glass wall. He could have kicked himself.

'You weren't,' he said quickly. 'It's just complicated. Law is the family business. My eldest brother's been carrying the firm ever since my father's first heart attack, more than ten years ago. I just need to do my share, you know?'

He held his breath for her next

question. Was this the moment he had to explain what else the family business embraced? Part of him thought, *Oh no, don't spoil today.* Part of him was almost relieved.

Hope relaxed, even smiled a little. But she didn't ask anything more. That precious moment of intimacy had gone.

5

Afterwards, Jonas was full of regret. The day had been spoilt anyway. Hope had retired behind what his grandmother would have called her party manners — polite, responsive, distant as the moon. Once the intimacy was gone, he had no idea how to get it back.

He told himself he was more thankful than ever that he hadn't succumbed to temptation and touched her. But he had a sneaking suspicion that he was just evading the issue. He even wondered whether she would come back the next day.

To his enormous relief, she did. But it was a mixed blessing. Marko, having arrived early to see a group of teenage scouts off on a forest adventure with their leaders, was firing on all cylinders when she arrived and hogged the conversation. And Hope didn't resort to party manners with him. She listened to the old ranger's stories with what looked like real interest, so that Marko ended up by flinging an arm round her and hugging her so hard that her toes nearly left the floor.

Jonas's hand clenched into a purposeful fist and he was half a second away from hurling the old lecher into the wall — only then he saw that Hope was laughing. She extracted herself from Marko's clinch, all right. But she wasn't offended and she didn't throw up that sea glass wall against the old ranger either.

Dammit, he couldn't be *jealous*! Marko was seventy if he was a day and had been his godfather's best friend. Jonas had known him since he was six.

He muttered something — he wasn't sure what — and went outside for some healthy fresh air and the space to turn back into his calm, civilized self again.

It took a while.

★ ★ ★

Hope watched Jonas walk out with mixed feelings. She wanted to be close to him, of course she did. When they were apart, she couldn't wait to see him again. Yet sometimes when she was with him, she would feel she couldn't breathe. It was exciting but at the same time, it felt as if she were out of control. Hope hadn't been out of control since she was eighteen, and didn't like it.

And sometimes, like yesterday, he would turn into a stranger all of a sudden. Then she would feel as if the ground had gone from under her, and she had no idea what to say to him or what to do. *He makes me feel shy*, she thought, disgusted with herself. *And I don't do shy!*

So she didn't follow him. Instead she stayed to welcome a party of excited primary school children and their teacher and watched Marko turn Moby into the straight man of a polished act. She even understood most of what he was saying. He spoke slowly, and the San Michele language was a ragbag of scraps from languages that Hope had encountered before.

When Jonas returned, she forgot that they had nearly fallen out yesterday and he'd made her feel shy, when he bent towards her with that enticing twinkle in his eyes. She felt herself blushing and pretended she wasn't as she muttered under her breath, 'I'm getting better at this language.'

Almost at once the teacher took a call on her mobile phone, listened, and then said loudly, '*Emergencia*.'

Jonas straightened at once and said in his own language, 'Quietly. The children!'

Marko faltered mid-story and then picked up the thread, as rapturous eyes stayed fixed on his face. Jonas had a low-voiced conversation with the teacher, then came back to Hope. No laughter in his eyes now.

'I need to borrow your 4×4.'

She jumped up. 'You won't be insured. I'll drive you wherever you need to go.'

He frowned but didn't waste time arguing. 'OK. But if we go off track,

I drive. Did you bring a waterproof? Blankets?'

Her heart jumped. 'Blankets, no. Will we need them?'

'Best to be prepared. Come with me.'

They went to the supply cupboard and he gave her a ranger's backpack and a couple of squashy kit bags. He shouldered a backpack of his own and dug out a thermal box so large that it would take both hands to carry it to the car. He stuffed a big military-looking two-way radio in one of the top pockets of his field jacket and a substantial rubber torch in the other.

'Try not to disturb the kids. With a bit of luck they'll think we're going on a picnic. Let's go.'

Hope's mouth was dry. Whatever had happened must be bad. That was a lot of rescue equipment.

'But what about Moby? I can't just leave him.'

'He'll be fine with Marko.' Over the top of the children's heads, he pointed to the dog and made a cradling gesture.

Marko gave them the thumbs-up and grinned. Jonas turned back to her. 'Satisfied?'

She nodded and followed him out to the car.

The children didn't even turn round to watch them go. Marko nodded at them over the top of the children's heads and made some signal. Jonas nodded. Marko smiled and continued reading. The teacher looked as if she were going to cry.

As soon as they were under way, Jonas got onto the radio. 'Klaus? We have a situation at the northeast boundary where the old oak came down in November. Peter took four Boy Scouts out there this morning and there was a ground movement. The fallen tree collapsed down the slope. One boy fell ten metres and isn't responding. Don't know how badly hurt he is. Peter and two others were trapped by the tree. Same for them. I'm on my way in Miss Kennard's vehicle.' And he pressed the button to receive an answer.

Hope, driving, could only marvel at how unemotional he sounded.

Klaus was equally calm. 'Marko is at base?' Beep.

'Yes.' Beep.

'Good. You should also know that there's a severe thunderstorm warning.' Beep.

'Got that,' said Jonas calmly. 'Severe storm. ETA?' Beep.

'No idea. Will tell Marko and get him to keep an eye on the alerts. See you there. Over and out.'

'Shit,' said Hope with feeling.

'We could have done without the thunder and lightning,' agreed Jonas. 'But the good news is that Peter and I've been doing one-on-one training with a bunch of mountain experts this week. So we're as good as we'll ever be.'

'Not in thunder and lightning, though.'

He smiled at her. 'We'll adapt. You'll see.'

And somehow she believed that they would.

His directions took her onto smaller tracks than the main one, but they were still on a distinctly beaten path when they came across a big green Land Rover Defender with the logo of the San Michele Forestry Commission on the side. Hope coasted to a halt behind it. Jonas swung out before she'd come to a full stop. She saw a figure pelting out from the trees to meet him. The newcomer looked about fifteen and very scared.

Jonas came back to her. 'They're not too far in. I'll reconnoitre and be right back.' They disappeared.

When they came back, Jonas was already talking on his radio. He shut it off when he came within hearing distance and Hope's heart sank.

'Bad?'

'Manageable, I think.'

'What can I do?'

'Dig the energy bars out of the backpacks, will you? The boys could do with them. I don't think Peter's broken anything, but I need to get him out from under a load of branches.' He went to the back and opened the kit bag she'd carried. 'Ah, here we are.'

She goggled. 'That's a chainsaw.'

'Only a very small one. Give the bars to Luka and wait here for Klaus.'

He disappeared again and soon she heard the whine of the saw. She winced, thinking of the poor guy who was underneath the tree that Jonas was sawing. She opened the big box and was not surprised to find a full first-aid kit. She recognized much of it from her time at the ski resort: a folding stretcher, head brace, packs of silver burn blankets and all types and sizes of bandages. And she had only picked over the top layer.

She looked up and saw the sky was darkening noticeably. 'Hurry,' she said under her breath.

Eventually three figures emerged from the trees. The first boy was not among them, she saw fearfully.

'Luka is staying at the site with Peter. The injured boy is his brother,' Jonas said reassuringly. 'He's not making sense, but he's conscious. Now that Peter's on his feet again, I can swing down on a rope and bring the boy up.'

The two boys climbed into the 4×4. Jonas showed them how to use one of the walkie-talkies and told them to keep in touch with Klaus. Jonas was very clear and patient. Hope saw that having something useful to do was steadying them.

A couple of big fat raindrops landed on the 4×4's hood with a splat. She saw Jonas's quick frown, but his steady, practical tone didn't change. He didn't even argue when she said that she was coming back to the accident site with him. 'There's too much for you to carry on your own, with ropes and the portable winch as well as the emergency stretcher.'

'I can't argue with that. Let's go.' He looped the coils of rope over his shoulder and picked up the winch. He wanted to carry the stretcher too, but Hope laughed at him.

'It's awkward, not heavy. I can manage.'

It was not easy walking. The forest floor was very uneven, sloping sharply downwards, and some of the scattered branches were as big as young trees. The fallen tree itself had torn up the earth. Half of its root system was now at right angles to the ground, looking like a gigantic old woman's head in a hairnet, with wisps of roots coming out at all angles. The top branches extended right over the gap where part of the hillside had collapsed.

Approaching, Hope saw that it looked as if a small chasm had opened up. Earth skittered away under her feet and tumbled down a slope that was nearly vertical.

'Don't go any closer,' said Jonas, still calm but very firm. 'The edge is still crumbling. I reckon that it's stable only as far as here.'

Comparatively stable, thought Hope. She didn't say so.

He urged her back to a safe distance

and went about setting up the tripod for the portable winch and making it secure. The boys helped; but Peter, it soon emerged, wasn't really functioning. He certainly wasn't going to be able to steady Jonas's weight on a rope. He was clearly in pain and had no strength in his arms at all.

Jonas looked at the sky, which was getting darker all the time. Rain, Hope thought, was going to erode that slope even further. She saw that Jonas had come to the same conclusion.

But even so: 'We'd better wait for Klaus,' he decided reluctantly.

Hope shook her head. 'I probably couldn't manage to stabilize your weight. But you could hold mine, couldn't you?'

'No.' Jonas looked suddenly furious.

It started to rain harder.

'I can swing on a rope,' she said steadily. 'And I know how to set up a foldable stretcher and strap someone onto it. We all did Red Cross courses in the ski resort. And it's going to rain *really* hard quite soon. And worse.'

He hated it. She could see he hated it. But also he had no real alternative. The boys were willing and sensible, but they just didn't have the necessary muscle. And through the edge of the trees, they could all see the storm approaching across the valley. The sky was a dense grey ceiling of cloud, lightning stabbed down intermittently, and there was the distant rumble of thunder following.

'Sooner the better, and get it over with?' she suggested.

Jonas swore. But he agreed. He had no choice.

She saw he was very pale, and patted his hand reassuringly. Then he took her through the drill to unfold the portable emergency stretcher, and working the straps and pulleys to fix it to the rope. He helped her put her arms through the straps so that she was effectively carrying it on her back. He helped her adjust the rope round herself and lean back into it.

'It's not difficult. Can be fun, in other circumstances. But try to move as little as you can. We don't know how stable this area is.'

She nodded. 'Thanks for the advice. I'll try to keep my head.'

'I know you will.'

And if that wasn't astonishing enough, as she lowered herself over the edge, he blew her a kiss. As if he meant it.

Hope tried to relax and minimize the swing. Jonas lowered her slowly, so that she managed to land close to the fallen boy. It was not very far. Before the land-slide, they could have walked the distance in a dozen steps.

Peter was leaning against the tree, valiantly reassuring the boy's brother and keeping in touch with the boys in the 4×4. Hope could hear him reporting to Jonas on all sorts of things from how near Klaus was getting in the rangers' vehicle, to which of the energy bars the boys liked best.

Jonas turned the winch handle when she asked, stopped when she told him.

He kept up a stream of clear instruction and advice. He made her laugh, too, even when the clatter of falling earth and stones got too frequent for comfort.

The boy was in a better condition than either of them had dared to hope. He was mumbling a bit, but he seemed to be making sense now. He'd clearly hurt his shoulder and ankle and scraped both legs, but his pupils were normal, and he responded to her questions sensibly. He even managed to roll onto the stretcher himself, though it was obviously painful.

When she got twitchy about the boy's condition, Jonas asked sensible questions and helped her take the right decisions. She buckled the boy tight onto the stretcher and called to Jonas to turn the winch. She stood on tiptoe to steady it as it rose. It was already only three feet or so from the top of the crater when it moved out of her grasp. As it disappeared over the top of the crater she laughed aloud in triumph.

One of the boys appeared at the edge.

He was clearly lying on his stomach. Too excited to remember his English, he talked in a jumble about *il maistre*, which sounded like poor Peter, Scout Leader, and something about *il principe*, which she thought might be the winch. But he grinned, so it clearly wasn't anything terrible.

The rain was falling hard now. Jonas sent down the rope again and winched her back to the top. The whole exercise had probably taken no more than twenty minutes.

He gave her a brief hug but said, 'We need to get the invalid to hospital. Klaus is about five minutes away. Will you be all right if I leave you here with Peter while Luka and I carry the stretcher up the hill to meet him?'

'Of course.'

The leader was half-leaning against the trunk of a tree. He was very pale. Hope thought he probably needed medical attention more than the injured boy did. He certainly needed painkillers. His right arm seemed to be hanging useless, and he seemed dazed.

Hope coiled up the rope neatly. The winch had come with printed instructions, so she began to dismantle that, too, while she watched Peter carefully out of the corner of her eye. She kept talking casually, though from time to time she asked him questions that he needed to answer. By the time Jonas returned, he had lost the dazed look.

'Klaus has gone. He's taking Luka and his brother to the rangers' centre. An ambulance is already on its way to meet them there,' said Jonas, taking over the dismantling and packing the winch away. 'Both boys seemed fine. The other two have moved into your vehicle, Peter. Ready to go?'

They helped Peter along between them. The rain was falling steadily now and was clearly going to get worse. Hope could feel the wet right through to her skin. She shivered.

The remaining two boys leaped out of the Scout leader's truck as soon as they saw him and took over helping him back to his vehicle.

'Is he going to be able to drive?' murmured Hope, concerned.

Jonas said briskly, 'Almost certainly not. I think he's dislocated that shoulder.'

'Then he'll need one of us to drive.'

Jonas laughed and shook his head, following the boys to Peter's truck. The leader was sitting in the passenger seat, drinking from a flask. He had a little more colour in his face.

'Brandy,' he said in heavily accented English, waving it at them. 'Klaus left it for us.' He nodded to Hope. 'He said to tell you, you were amazing.'

'Thank you. About driving you home . . . '

But Jonas shook his head. 'No need.' He said something to the leader, clearly translating. They both laughed heartily.

'What?' she said, bristling but sticking to her guns. 'If he can't drive . . . '

'Darling Hope, he has the company of two teenage boys, both of whom are just dying to drive that thing.'

'But . . . '

'And are perfectly competent to do so.' Then in his own language she guessed he said, 'Get going. We'll follow as soon as I've stowed the gear.'

The Scout leader nodded. He raised his hand with a manifest effort in a gesture of farewell. 'Thank you, signorina. I hope we see you again. Let's go, boys.'

Hope and Jonas made for the Antons' 4×4. But Hope saw over her shoulder that both boys were grinning. One scrambled into the back of the cabin, while the other leaped into the driving seat. He handled the steering wheel with serene confidence, Hope saw, and he started the truck smoothly. As it passed the 4×4, he turned his head and gave them a cheeky grin.

'Told you,' murmured Jonas.

He opened the passenger door of the Antons' 4×4 and rummaged in the back seat for the dog blanket. 'You're shivering. You need to get out of your wet things. And have a swig of this.'

Jonas opened the flask. The top was the size of a shot glass, made of silver. He splashed a generous tot of brandy into it and passed it across to her.

'Drink. It will warm you up. Try and dry off as much as you can. I'll be back.'

Before she could answer, he had turned and run back into the trees to collect the rest of the equipment. It took him two journeys.

Hope didn't like brandy, but she had a couple of sips and had to admit it warmed her up. She hauled off her waterproof and pulled the blanket off the back seat to huddle round her. It smelled richly of Moby, but it was warm and familiar. She only realized her hands had been shaking convulsively once the trembling stopped.

Jonas opened the driver's door and got in just as the thunder started in earnest. Silently Hope handed him the flask. He tipped it down his throat as if it were cough medicine and let out a long breath.

'Well,' he said, 'we did all right.'

It was such a huge understatement that she laughed aloud at that. 'Yes, we did.'

For a moment she thought they might kiss. But then he seemed to pull an invisible jacket round him and turned towards the steering wheel. 'Right. I'm driving, no argument. I know these tracks, and the weather is getting worse all the time. Let's get you home.'

She could only feel relieved. 'First we have to pick up Moby,' she reminded him.

He nodded. 'It's on the way.'

He put the car in motion, driving slowly along a track where the potholes were turning into pools and the track was disappearing into mud. The thunder was getting worse, too, right overhead now. Then suddenly there was a sizzle of lightning that made them both jump and almost blinded them. It was followed by a huge groaning sound, and for a moment Hope thought that the track was going to cave in as the woodland floor had done. But when they'd gone another five or six hundred metres, they saw what had caused the noise. A huge tree had fallen sideways, scattering branches all over the track. It was still reverberating.

It completely blocked the way. Great trees rose on either side of the track, caging them in. Hope saw at once that there was no possibility of going off road here.

Jonas stopped the engine and sat there for some minutes in silence. He looked not just drawn and tired, but utterly defeated. 'I should never have got you into this,' he muttered.

Hope wanted to put her arms round him. She didn't but said, 'Don't look so worried. We're OK. The car is upright and still functioning. I've no doubt Marko will look after Moby for as long as it takes. We can just stay here and sit out the storm.'

He drummed his hands on the steering wheel. 'We may have to. Though it's not really a good idea. If only I could *think* . . . '

'How far away is that fire tower?'

He shook his head. 'Too far. But good thinking. Maybe . . . '

He fished the walkie-talkie out of his pocket. Marko took a while to answer, but when he did, Jonas outlined their situation. The radio crackled.

Jonas raised his voice. 'Those forest ecologists had a hut somewhere round here, didn't they? Where is it?'

Hope couldn't make out what Marko replied, but it seemed to make sense to Jonas.

'Thanks. I'll look.'

The rain was coming down in sheets now. The sky above the trees was as black as night. Hope had no idea what the time was, but she was sure that it was early evening at the latest.

Jonas pulled out a map of the forest from under the dash and spread it over the wheel. 'Ah,' he said with satisfaction, 'that might work.' He folded the map. 'When the rain eases up, I'm going to look for the researchers' field hut. It should be down this road and off to the left. If it's accessible, I'll come and get you.'

'I'll come too,' said Hope firmly.

'No, you won't,' he said even more firmly. 'The ground could be treacherous. I've known these woods since I was a kid. I know the signs. You don't.'

'But — '

He turned a ravaged face to her. 'Please let me do this. I *need* to. When I sent you off down that rope — '

'Oh, *Jonas*.' She couldn't say any more. She was too choked. But it was enough.

'Thank you,' he said simply.

They sat in shattered silence until the torrent abated somewhat. Then he pulled the zip of his jacket up his throat, dragged the hood over his head, switched on the big torch and slid out of the vehicle.

Hope prepared for a worrying vigil, but Jonas was back inside ten minutes. She was so relieved that she could have kissed him. This time, as he closed the driver's door behind him, she did hug him. Awkwardly, but it was a real hug. It felt strange.

He laughed. It was pure triumph. 'I've found us a roof over our heads.'

He patted her arm, but his mind was already on ways and means, she could see. She drew back, hugging the blanket around her.

He switched on the engine and put the car in gear. Just for a moment he assessed the track, then sent her a look every bit as mischievous as the teenage driver's had been. 'Buckle up. It's going to be a bumpy ride.'

She did. And it was.

In spite of that wicked look, he drove with extreme care. He reversed slowly, then went off the track and they were weaving their way between large trees interwoven with undergrowth, so it was impossible to see the forest floor. A couple of times the 4×4 wallowed like a boat in high seas. It took all of Hope's self-control not to gasp aloud. But she told herself that the only thing she could do to help was *not* to break his concentration. So she folded her lips together and kept quiet until they stopped outside a small cabin.

Violent rain pattered off the trees like machine-gun fire. The windscreen wipers couldn't keep up with it. As the engine died, she heard thunder, really close, and shivered.

Jonas pulled her discarded waterproof back round her shoulders protectively. 'This is as close as I can get. Now we run.'

They barrelled through the door and he slammed it shut behind them. Water cascaded off them as if they'd run through a waterfall. She heard the drips, but the cabin was in complete darkness. She couldn't see her own hand in front of her face. She heard the weather outside; her own breathing. His. Suddenly she couldn't remember how to breathe anymore. She put out a hand to steady herself. And found Jonas. He was closer than she'd realized.

Or had she known in her bones exactly how close he was?

He hauled her into his arms and kissed her hard. His lips were cold but his kiss burned. Her body responded instantly. Her skin was icy but inside she was hot. And hungry.

Oh yes, she'd known, all right.

Hope kissed him back with abandon.

★   ★   ★

Take it at her pace.

The little voice was there in the back of his head but Jonas couldn't help himself. His arms tightened. It didn't feel like a first kiss. It felt as if they were already lovers, as if they'd done this a hundred times before.

In the dark they kissed until they had to stop or suffocate.

Hope backed off a little, not as if she were pulling away, just reaching for some air. She leaned back in his arms and gave a huge, satisfied sigh. Then, unexpectedly, she began to laugh.

'What?' he said, instantly on his guard.

But Hope was gleeful. He could hear it in her voice. 'Togetherness is smelling of the same dog blanket.'

Jonas groaned. 'I'd forgotten the dog blanket. Did you have to remind me?' He sniffed theatrically. 'Unmistakably Moby.' Then he too started to laugh.

It was infectious. Hope started again. After that, of course, neither of them could stop. They hooted and snorted and clung to each other until their lungs hurt and their eyes streamed.

'Oh, I ache,' she gasped eventually, arms round his neck, her head against his chest.

At once Jonas was conscience-stricken. He stopped laughing. 'Did you hurt yourself on that damn rope?'

'No, no,' she said in reassurance.

But she was shaking convulsively. It was faint but unmistakable. He could feel her whole body quivering as he held her. 'Shock. I should have thought of that.' He rubbed her arms with vigour, remorseful. 'Damn it, I ought to get you back to civilization, with a warm bath and a decent meal.'

'Well, that's not going to happen any time soon, is it? We'll just have to make the best of it.' She sounded surprisingly cheerful about it, he thought.

He let her go reluctantly and said, 'I'll scout around and see what I can find.'

He brought a slim pencil torch out of a back pocket and ran it over the walls. The place looked more solid than he remembered. He set off to explore and Hope came with him, which he didn't expect, her hand tucked into his as if it was the most natural thing in the world. Was it for warmth? Maybe she just didn't want to be left alone in case of spiders and other wildlife.

Or was this her way of telling him that her pace had accelerated? He was almost dizzy at the thought. His hand tightened painfully round hers. She laughed softly and squeezed back.

Jonas said at random, 'There's a stack of logs. So there must be a fireplace somewhere.'

131

'Good,' said Hope. 'I've been making fires since I was a child. I'll soon get a blaze going.'

She did, too, once they found the chimney, an elderly brick structure cleared and cleaned, and obviously still in working order.

The scientists had added major amenities to the old shepherd's hut they had colonized. There was a kitchen and even a basic laboratory of sorts, though the bottled gas that powered both seemed to have run out. More important, there were bunk beds with bedding in large vacuum storage bags and a supply of wine, and ring-pull cans of nuts and crackers.

'Carpet picnic,' said Hope gleefully, looking up from her attentions to the fire when Jonas revealed the stash.

The floor had no carpet but, unzipped, the vacuum bags gave up four top-quality sleeping bags and several felt blankets. Jonas built them a serviceable shelter against the draughts, while Hope set out their meal on the hearth. Jonas brought enough logs from the store to keep the fire in until morning.

There were neither plates nor glasses, but they used the scientists' solid earthenware mugs for both. And when the fire was blazing steadily, Hope took off her wet things and wrapped herself in one of the blankets, while she draped them over whatever she could find to dry.

'You too?' she said to Jonas.

It didn't seem like a momentous decision. His outer things were already steaming gently. He stripped and swathed himself in an Aztec-patterned blanket, which made her laugh gently. He sat down again, stretching and leaning on his elbow, and watched her drying her hair in front of the flames.

'You seem a practised camper. Family holidays? Girl Guide?' he enquired lazily, pouring them both more wine.

She shook the draggled curls. 'Not a chance. Not my mother's scene at all.'

She thought about it. 'In fact the only really practical advice my mother ever gave me was not to go on a date without my running-away money.'

He choked. 'Really?'

'Really. All my survival skills are things I've learned since I left home. Actually, that was probably the reason I had to leave home, now I come to think about it. Otherwise I'd have been completely useless.'

'I can't imagine that.' He reached out and captured a strand of damp hair, winding it round his finger.

She didn't move away. His blood started to murmur persistently.

'Oh I was heading straight for parasite of the parish, believe me. I was rubbish at school, had no idea what I wanted to do. And my mother just thought girls found husbands and that was them settled.' She pushed her hair back, moving out of the direct heat of the fire, and stretched out companionably beside him. 'My friend Ally always knew she was going to be a writer, but then she was brilliant,' she said reflectively. 'And my other best friend cooked like an angel. But me, no. I was useless at everything.'

Her blanket was slipping off her shoulder as she curled into his nest of accumulated sleeping bags. Did she know?

'And now?' he said, distracted.

'I seem to be quite good at sorting out problems. Even crises. A boss once told me I hit the ground running. I can drive just about anything. Pick up languages.'

'I remember. The first time we met. You had a really good go at the San Michele dialect.'

'Fluent up to bottom of page 6 of the phrasebook.' She held out her mug for more wine. 'I like this stuff.'

'San Michele's finest.'

'Really?'

He turned the bottle round and looked at it. 'Well, no. Good supermarket middle rank, though.'

She raised her mug in a solemn toast.

'Here's to the scientists, God bless them. How many bottles did they leave, by the way?'

He was amused. 'Are you saying you want me to open another?'

'Eventually,' said Hope composedly. And kissed him.

Hope, he found, was an interested but not very expert lover. She seemed astonished by his desire to please her. She arched under his slow, appreciative touch, eyes tight shut, and muttered, 'What are you *doing*?'

'This is what I call the full-body kiss,' said Jonas, enjoying himself hugely.

She moaned. 'Don't tease.'

'Then don't rush.'

Her eyes opened indignantly at that, but then she stopped, head pressed against his chest, listening. 'I know your heartbeat,' she said, awed. 'I'd know it anywhere.'

He couldn't speak. To be fair, he didn't exactly lose control. But after that, he didn't waste time telling Hope not to rush any more.

They never got to the neat bunks. They stayed in front of the firelight and made love and hugged and laughed and made love some more.

And when she fell asleep in his arms, he looked down at the corkscrew curls, most of which he had played with, and felt he had been given the world.

* * *

The next morning Jonas woke first. Hope was lying on her front, one arm possessively across his chest. He lay there looking at the smoke-stained ceiling, idly stroking her hand. She muttered something but didn't wake. He grinned and dropped a light kiss on her shoulder. It was cold.

This was where a chivalrous knight would get out of bed and attend to the fire, so his lady didn't have to shiver when she woke. Oh well, he might as well get on with it, then. He raised her hand and carefully tucked it under the tangle of blankets and sleeping bags.

The embers were still glowing, so he brought them back to life with some twigs from the log basket. When he was sure they had caught, he carefully added just one small log and watched it while he pulled last night's clothes on. They were cold and stiff. So when he was sure the first log had caught, he collected Hope's underwear, shirt and trousers, and arranged them in front of the fire.

He looked at his watch. Later than he'd thought. There would be someone at the rangers' centre by now. He put another, bigger log on the fire; then took the walkie-talkie outside so as not to disturb Hope, and tried to raise them. It took a few minutes while he prowled round the hut, discovering a stream, running fast after last night's storm, and more fallen branches. Eventually Marko answered.

'Jonas? How you doing?'

'Broke into the scientists' hut successfully, thank you. Hope's asleep.'

'Not surprised. She did well yesterday.'

'She did, didn't she?' Jonas realized he felt proud of her. He wondered how she would feel about that. Probably annoyed, he thought, laughing gently at both of them.

Marko said, 'What do the trails look like? I'll put it on the whiteboard.'

Jonas ran through what he could see and what he remembered from last night's journey. 'I reckon we've been lucky.'

'Too right.'

'Now that I can actually see out of the windscreen, I should be able to get us back to the centre. No idea what time, though.'

Marko laughed. 'Let the lass sleep. She'll be exhausted.'

Jonas narrowed his eyes at the instrument suspiciously. Then he realized that Marko was talking about Hope's heroic rope trick of the day before. He laughed silently, this time just at himself. But it had reminded him.

'How's the boy? Have you heard?'

'Under observation. That's all so far.

But he was talking coherently by the time they got him here.'

'Great. Let's hope he carries on getting better. As for us, I'll call if we need help. Unless I do, we'll see you later.'

'Good. That dog of Hope's is wearing me out. You can tell her he made himself at home,' said Marko with feeling.

'I'll do that. Thanks. Cheers.'

Jonas went back into the hut. Hope was groggily sitting up, wild red hair everywhere and blankets slipping deliciously. He hurriedly closed the door. It was cold outside.

'Awake?'

She yawned massively, eyes tight shut. 'Getting there.'

'I've reported in. Marko says that the boy you rescued is better this morning. They've kept him in hospital for observation.'

'*We* rescued.' She rubbed her eyes. 'Oh, that's good. What about the others?'

'Sounded OK, from what he was saying.'

'Did he think to say how Moby is?'

Jonas grinned. 'Made himself very comfortable from the sound of it. Marko sounded a bit shell-shocked.'

She gave a choke of sleepy laughter. 'He does like plenty of exercise. I suppose we ought to go and collect him as soon as possible.'

She sounded almost reluctant, he thought. His pulse speeded up. To comfort himself as much as her he said, 'Well don't get cold. We can take our time. The dog's safe enough with Marko, and I'm going to see if there's any way this place can rise to coffee.'

Her eyes flared open at that. 'You're serious?'

'I've got a hunch. There's a stream outside, so we have water. I'm going to have a rummage through their cupboards. Would you like coffee if I can find any?'

She groaned eloquently. It was disturbingly reminiscent of some memorable moments last night. He swallowed hard and found that her eyes were fixed on

him, green and mischievous. She pulled
the blankets up round her bare shoulders with a deliberately voluptuous shiver.

Chivalrous knight, he reminded himself, breaking out in a cold sweat.

She laughed and let him go. Sort of.
'Any chance of a shower?'

He shook his head. There was a basic
bathroom but it was out of water. He'd
looked. 'You could take a dip in the
stream if you really want to. It will be
very cold. But . . . '

She shook her head and leaned back
among the tumbled covers. The witch-
green eyes were dancing. 'I'll just lie
here and wait then, shall I?'

Glug. Jonas fled to the rudimentary
kitchen in case he started to beat his
breast and roar like a gorilla.

But he forgot that in the delight of
finding that the scientists were better
stocked than he had discovered last
night. Not only did they have coffee in
small freeze-dried packs, but there were
several other packs that he recognized
labelled 'Space Food'. Even better,

there was a barbecue tray on legs that had clearly been used to heat stuff over the fire, and a heavy-bottomed pan. He bounded back to Hope with his treasure trove.

'You can have,' he said, consulting his haul, 'scrambled eggs, porridge, boeuf bourguignon, or apple crumble.'

'Don't torture me.'

'It's true.' He waved a pack under her nose. 'Freeze-dried food like astronauts have. Just add boiling water.'

She looked at him in awe. 'Is there anything you don't know?'

'Well, in this case, I've had personal experience. You get them in science museums. My brother's kids go crazy for them.'

'My hero.'

He kissed her lightly. 'You make me feel ten feet tall.' He was only half-joking.

He built up the fire and brought out the ingredients and a couple of additional mugs. 'For the space goo,' he explained, setting them down.

Hope was buttoning her shirt, but she looked up and stared at him with odd concentration for a moment. 'You warmed my clothes for me.'

'Yes.'

'Thank you.'

It was all she said, but it felt momentous. They sat side by side watching the water boil. The scrambled egg turned out to be apple crumble, but it was quite tasty apple crumble, as Hope said, so they shared the pack. They held hands while they drank their coffee. Not speaking, they sat and watched the flames die down. Hope put her head on his shoulder.

'How are you feeling now?' he murmured.

'Pretty damn good. You?'

Ten feet tall. 'Likewise.'

6

Jonas had intended to see Hope home to the Antons' villa, but the rangers really wanted him to go to the hospital. The injured boy was asking for him, they said. He didn't ask her to go with him and, anyway, she wanted a shower before she did anything else. And she needed to get Moby home and fed.

'I bet Marko's been giving him biscuits,' she said, observing the dog racing round in wild circles. 'I don't blame him. Moby has a very good line in starving dog when there are human biscuits around. He'll probably throw up at some point. My brother warned me about that.'

'Good point,' said Jonas, not arguing.

He came out of the rangers' centre to see her to the 4×4, but he didn't kiss her. Well, the rangers would have seen, she supposed. She didn't really mind.

She was floating about three feet above the ground in a sweetly scented pink cloud. And anyway, he squeezed her hand in *that* way and looked pleased when she blushed.

'I'll call you. And anyway, I'll see you tomorrow,' he said.

'You will.'

She found she was singing in the car.

It was late afternoon by the time she got back. Moby rushed round the house to say hello to every room, his claws clattering on the parquet flooring, giving little excited barks. Then he collapsed in the kitchen and lay on his back, snoring loudly. His paws quivered as he dreamed.

'Sometimes,' Hope told his unconscious form, 'you can be very human.'

He reminded her of her father, collapsed on the study sofa after Sunday lunch, with the newspaper sliding gently to the floor, snoring in exactly the same way. She smiled. For all his mistakes, there had been something about her father that was innocent and very sweet.

Hope fully expected to find anxious messages from Poppy and Mrs Anton wondering about her silence. But there were none. So she took a photograph of the slumbering Moby and sent it to them with a reassuring text, just in case. And then she showered and washed her hair at last.

She was curled up on the couch in the den, wearing a guest bathrobe with her hair in a towel, when Jonas called.

'How are you feeling now?'

Wonderful. Like live electricity. And a bit strange.

She didn't say that. It felt too new and just a little embarrassing. She said, 'Clean, actually. I left enough twiggery and bits of leaf on the floor of the shower to start a small compost heap.'

Jonas seemed to have no problems with embarrassment or strangeness at all. 'I'm sorry I wasn't there to see that.'

Hope wriggled her bare toes under a cushion. 'How was the patient?'

'Patched up and doing well. A bit

subdued. Peter had told the boys to stick together and stay close behind him, and our patient deliberately shot off on his own.'

'Exploring?'

'More likely to have a smoke.'

'Ah.'

'Nobody's admitting it, but he and his brother both look as if they've got bad consciences and their mother was hopping mad when I was at the hospital.'

'Then you're probably right. And Peter?'

'Swearing about the pain. But he won't take painkillers, so he has to put up with it. He says he'll be back for training tomorrow morning.'

'So all's well that ends well.'

'Yes, thank God.' His voice roughened. He might almost be the one in pain, not Peter.

Hope remembered how, when Jonas had said, 'When I sent you off down that rope,' how anguished he'd looked, and for a moment she couldn't speak.

She wished passionately that he were there with her; that she could tell him to come over, *now*, and they could comfort each other. But it was no good. She didn't know how to say it without sounding, well, hysterical.

'Hope? Are you still there?'

She swallowed an obstruction in her throat. 'Still here.'

'What are you doing with the rest of the evening?'

Missing you. 'Drying my hair, watching a movie with a happy ending, going to bed early.'

He groaned. 'Sounds just about perfect. Wish I was there with you.'

'So do I.'

There was a little silence. Then he said carefully, 'Don't say that if you don't mean it.'

Hope swallowed. 'I do mean it.'

There was an even longer silence. 'No. I *can't.*' Jonas sounded as if he was in pain. 'I've got to write my bit of the report and then put the whole thing into a file for Klaus to sign tomorrow.

And draft a press release. And be responsible.'

'Yes.'

'Tomorrow. I'll see you tomorrow?'

'Yes.'

'Promise?'

'I can be in the forest by dawn,' she said fervently.

Jonas gave a shaken laugh. 'That will be interesting.'

Hope's toes curled in sympathy. 'Won't it just?'

They both talked for longer than they needed, saying nothing important, just for the sheer pleasure of his voice in her ear, his breathing at the other end. A message came up on the screen that she had a text, another, and then there was a call waiting. It was Poppy's number.

'There's a call I really ought to take.'

But she was reluctant to let him go. And so was he. Half-laughing at themselves, they talked farewell nonsense until he finally drew it to a close with a little crooning noise, somewhere between a kiss and a lullaby.

In the ensuing silence, Hope sat grinning like a loon and hugging the phone. She was as warm and rumpled as if Jonas had just walked out of the room.

'This,' she said aloud, trying to be sensible and not really managing it, 'is a new experience.'

By that time, of course, Poppy's call had gone to voicemail. Not very successfully, either. The sound kept cutting out, so that Hope could only make out one word in three. And when she tried to call back, she got the out of service message.

The house telephone rang. 'Hello?'

But even that was not a good line. Poppy had difficulty making herself heard through the crackle of static and a persistent buzzing. 'Oh, Hope, I'm sorry . . . trying and trying to call . . . no signal . . . terrible storms . . . '

'Here too,' said Hope, realizing with relief that there was no point in trying to explain her overnight absence on a line like this. 'Here too. Moby is fine.'

'What?' Poppy was clearly shouting for all she was worth, but it was very hard to hear.

Hope raised her voice and enunciated clearly. 'I said we've had bad thunder and lightning here too.'

There were more squeaks and then Mrs Anton came on the line. She was worried about the house and its power supply.

Hope reassured her that the villa was still standing and recognized an opportunity to seek permission to invite Jonas to the house. 'I've met a forest ranger when I was walking Moby. Would it be OK to ask him back here for a meal?'

Mrs Anton was delighted. ' . . . so glad . . . Blake must know him . . . name? . . . local? . . . stay if you want . . . '

'Thank you,' said Hope with real gratitude. 'Jonas Reval. He's a volunteer from the capital.'

' . . . again?'

'Volunteer,' she shouted into the

chittering handset. 'Reval.'

But Mrs Anton was already talking again. As far as Hope could make out, Mrs Anton was telling her to ask volunteer ranger Reval to stay in the spare room as long as he wanted to, while the storms lasted. It would comfort Mrs Reval to think that Hope was not on her own if there should be a tornado or similar extreme weather event.

Hope was startled. 'Do you think that's likely?'

But Mrs Anton had become inaudible. Then the line went dead before the handset started up its grating 'off the hook' noise.

Hope put it back in the dock. Neither Poppy nor Mrs Anton called back.

The conversation and mechanical noises had woken Moby. So she gave him a head rub and then let him out into the garden for a healthful gallop round the perimeter before bed.

She left the kitchen door open, sending a shaft of light into the pitch darkness outside, while she refilled his water bowl and made herself a warm drink to take to bed. She had the vague feeling that there was something she ought to have noticed, something she should have done or said. But tiredness was beginning to catch up with her, and she just couldn't quite focus on the specific issue. Oh well, if it was important she would remember it in the morning.

So when Moby thundered back in and flung himself on his water bowl and then his kitchen couch, Hope locked and bolted the doors, switched off the lights, and took her phone and mug of camomile tea up to bed.

The camomile infusion was still there, undrunk, in the morning. But her memory was back. And it brought her awake and out of bed in alarm.

Jonas had said — surely he had said? — that he was writing a press release about the rescue. A press release! Hope had been on the receiving end of press attention in the past and she really didn't want to go there again. She needed to speak to him. Urgently.

She called. He answered at once. 'Good morning, sweetness.' She could hear the smile in his voice.

'Um, hello.' For a moment Hope forgot what she needed to say in the sheer physical pleasure of having him murmur into her ear. She shivered voluptuously.

'Sleep well? No ill effects from our adventure?'

That brought her back to reality. 'I'm fine. Have you published your press release yet?'

'No.' There was a half-question in his voice.

'I was wondering — I mean, do you have to mention me in it?'

'You're not going to be mentioned,' he said very firmly. 'I've already told Klaus.'

She gave a great huff of relief, sinking back onto the side of the bed like a sack of abandoned laundry. 'Why Klaus?'

'I'm a volunteer,' he reminded her. 'I only did the first draft because I was actually there during most of it. But the rangers have to decide what they want going out under their name.'

'Oh. I see. Of course.'

'Don't worry. Klaus isn't going to mention you in the press release. This is about a forest event and safety, not some human interest story.'

'Are you sure?'

'Yes.' It was somehow more calming than any amount of reassuring argument would have been.

Relieved, she moved on to the Next Big Thing on her agenda. 'I talked to the Antons last night. It was a terrible line. But I asked and she's given me permission to ask you over. You're even invited to stay, in case there's a tornado and I need protection.' She was really proud of how casually amused she sounded.

Jonas laughed. 'I can handle that. Tonight?'

At once Hope was flustered. 'What?'

'I've got training all morning. You can bring Moby over this afternoon and we'll walk through the forest as normal. Then I'll take you out to dinner afterwards and we'll return to the Villa Anton for some serious tornado drill.'

Hope swallowed a couple of times. 'That would be nice.'

It would not be nice. It would be amazing. And wonderful. And terrifying. And completely new.

I am so out of my depth now.

'Great. See you later.'

Hope told herself that it was the same as any other day in San Michele. Only of course it wasn't. For one thing, the morning ritual didn't happen. Presumably the Antons were still having connection difficulties. For another, Moby was restless, demanding first attention, then a walk, then wanting to go back to the house.

'The sooner I get you into the forest the better,' she told him.

So she got to the rangers' centre while Jonas and Peter were still in discussion with their tutors of the morning.

'They won't be long,' said Klaus, who was looking very smart in a tailored uniform. 'Fire protocols evaluation. Formality, really.'

'No problem. We're early. Moby can't seem to settle.'

'Ah well, dogs don't like their routine interrupted. Any more than rangers do,' he added with a twinkle. 'I'm off to the capital to explain myself for permitting a lightning strike in their forest.' He didn't sound too bothered, though.

Hope laughed and wished him luck as he went off.

It meant that Jonas was left alone in charge of the rangers' centre and had to stay close.

'So I'll be a volunteer ranger's volunteer assistant,' she said, pleased.

Under his instruction, she helped file and dust exhibits, tidied the rubbish dump that was the stationery cabinet, and even checked that the handwritten whiteboard messages, photographed daily, had all been transposed to the computerized diary. She took Moby for several walks, making sure that they stayed strictly on the signposted trails. And she held the fort while Jonas took a couple of academics from the university to look at the landslip. They returned soaked by the steady downpour.

'Right,' Jonas said, returning from seeing them off and shaking rainwater out of his eyes, 'I'll just divert incoming calls to my cell and we can go to dinner. I don't think there's any fire that would have a chance in rain like this.'

He took her to a roadhouse on the shores of a lake she hadn't seen before. It had a plain wooden floor, unvarnished wooden tables and a cheerful air of casual busy-ness. A multi-generational family group were seated in the middle, where several tables had been pushed together. They were clearly celebrating.

Jonas ushered Hope and Moby to a booth along the side wall and raised a hand to a jeans-clad waitress as he slid in opposite.

'Busy tonight,' he said in English when the woman came over to them.

She nodded. 'Wedding anniversary from over the border. They've brought their own music.'

Hope smiled at her. 'Will it be good?'

The woman flashed her a grin, recognizing a fellow world traveller. 'They've promised not to yodel. That's all I know.'

The food was simple and well-cooked, with a hint of herbs that Hope didn't recognize but found intriguing. By the time they'd finished eating, a three-piece band did indeed start up with a wild gipsyish tune. The waitress had pushed tables to one side so the family could take to the floor in a big circle dance. Hope watched, fascinated.

'What is it? Do you know?' she asked Jonas.

He groaned. 'Oh yes. We all had to learn it at primary school. What a Spanish friend of mine calls *muy tipico, muy folklorico*. It goes on forever.'

Other diners were beginning to join in. The circle broke into two, with much laughter.

'Can we?'

'If you want to.'

She hesitated. 'Is it difficult?'

Jonas smiled into her eyes. 'Not if you hold my hand and let me drive.'

She smiled right back and stood up as if she were floating about six inches above the floor. 'Whatever you say.'

Moby put his nose on his paws and sighed deeply.

They joined the dance. Jonas held her hand tightly, twirled her energetically when appropriate, and rescued her when she started to go the wrong way. They ended breathless but unbruised except, as Jonas pointed out, from enthusiastic back-slapping from the family and their friends.

'Apart from that, I call it a hundred percent success. We stayed upright!'

'It was fun,' Hope said when she got her breath back.

Jonas laughed. 'Ah, but this version definitely comes with a family viewing certificate.'

'What do you mean?'

His smile was bland. 'There's a more — er — authentic version. The women form an inner circle and go clockwise and the men circle outside them, going counterclockwise. You're supposed to dance it on May morning under a linden tree to welcome spring and new life. Goes faster and faster.'

'Sounds as if it would make you dizzy.'

'That's the whole point. When the music crashes out, the boys all chase the girl they want to catch. Lot of bruises in that one. Some couples have disappeared for days, too.' His hand tightened. 'Speaking of which . . . '

Under the table, Moby sat up, alert.

Jonas did not look at the dog. His eyes were intent and very, very serious.

Hope caught her breath. 'Yes. Let's go home.'

Outside it was quite dark now, with scudding clouds blocking out the moon. She thought he would take her back to the rangers' centre to pick up the Antons' car, but he drove straight to the villa. They tore through narrow lanes she had never seen before. She thought that a couple of times he even shot off road completely, though she couldn't be sure. The headlights made a tunnel ahead of them and they seemed to flash through it. His breathing was ragged. They didn't speak.

It didn't take long. At the villa he drove round to the back and stopped. Moby sat up with an excited little bark. Jonas killed the headlights and jumped out to let the dog out. As Moby raced joyously off into the darkness of the garden, Jonas turned to Hope.

'Just tell me one thing.'

'Anything.'

'You don't sleep with the dog.'

She walked into his arms, half-laughing, half-shaking with need. 'The dog sleeps in the kitchen.'

His arms closed round her, hard as steel. 'Thank God for that.'

She unlocked the kitchen door and they went inside. 'We'll have to wait until Moby's tired himself out,' she said apologetically. 'Otherwise he howls in the middle of the night.'

He kissed her lingeringly. 'Whatever. By the way, I meant to ask — did you get to look at the press release?'

She shook her head. So he brought out his smartphone and called up the page on the forest website. It just said that one person had been slightly injured but it didn't have a word about the rescue.

Hope let out a little puff of relief. 'I hadn't realized how jumpy that made me,' she said almost to herself.

Jonas nodded. 'Do you want to talk about it? Tell me why, maybe?'

She hesitated. She'd taken a policy decision years ago never to try to hide her father's chequered history. Well, she had told Jonas about it, first chance she got. But the effect on her teenage self, especially when a couple of journalists targeted her — that was different. She hated thinking about it, much less telling anyone. It made her feel weak and needy and oddly ashamed.

There had been a photograph of her, an awkward fourteen in her first full-length gown, at the birthday party of one of the girls at her posh boarding school. The tabloids had bought it from the so-called friend and regularly trotted it out whenever they did a piece on her father's crime. *Sir Gerald Kennard and his socialite daughter* was the usual caption. The story would hint that her father had defrauded all those people while he went to their parties so that Hope could live a celebrity lifestyle. And of course some people had believed it.

She tried to explain it now, haltingly. 'The crazy thing is, I hated the big dances. Still do. Won't go near them. And I'm never wearing a ball gown again.' She swallowed. 'Someone spat at me in the street once.'

Jonas was appalled.

'Not in the village, of course. My mother had taken me to town, shopping. That was always her comfort recreation.' She gave an unhappy smile.

'She whisked me away of course. Told me it wasn't my fault. Nobody who knew me would believe the stories that the papers were printing. But it gave me a bit of a phobia about the press. And I'm still not great about going into clothes shops.'

He hugged her. 'I'm not surprised.'

She rested her head against his shoulder. It felt good. She could almost feel the old hurt slide away. At least she could look at it now without wincing. Maybe she could even probe a little deeper . . .

'I had to change schools. I was glad to get away, to be honest. I didn't like boarding school. The girls were cliquey and their mothers all hated mine. She was a bit of a flirt, to be fair, and the fathers probably made too much of a fuss of her. But then, when I went to the local school, there were a couple of photographers who hung round the gates, trying to get a shot of me looking miserable. They wanted to publish some stupid story about me getting my comeuppance, my brother said.'

'And did they?'

Hope gave a hard laugh. 'No. I went into school every day with a manic grin on my face and came out the same. So they never got the shot they wanted. But just having them hanging round made some of the people at my new school think I was a — well, a spoilt wannabe celebrity, like they said.'

That had been almost the worst time. Hope hated remembering it. If it hadn't been for Ally and then Flora, she would have wanted to die.

Jonas sat like a rock, his shoulder steady and somehow homelike.

Hope rubbed her face against the cloth of his jacket. 'It's kind of made me want to duck whenever anyone points a camera at me.'

'And I suppose that's why no Facebook page or anything?'

'Yes. I got used to having no social media presence, and then I didn't miss it. I email my mates. I've never wanted to go back.'

'Do journalists still hound you?'

'Not really. Sometimes someone digs a bit when there's a new fraud case and wants to know what happened to us. My brother tells me about it. He has to have a Facebook page, Twitter, Instagram, the works. He runs a landscape gardening outfit and needs it for his business. So they get in touch with him. Or they go to the village pub and try to dig some dirt. The landlord runs them out.'

'Is that why you don't go back home?'

'No. That's just me wanting to find out who I am.'

'You mean apart from the paparazzi's victim?'

Hope shook her head. 'Apart from the under-educated girl with no idea what she was good at or what she wanted to do,' she corrected.

'But it still hurts.' He sounded really tense, as if it mattered to him. As if he couldn't bear what had happened to her.

She wanted to comfort him. 'Hey,' she said. 'It was a long time ago.' And realized that it was true. She stopped nestling in his shoulder and reached up to bring his mouth down to hers. 'Let's get the dog in and go to bed,' she whispered.

They did. She pulled out Moby's bed from the cupboard, then locked the kitchen door and hid the key where Mrs Anton had told her, all on autopilot.

They went upstairs hand in hand.

Hope felt a moment of strangeness when they went into her shadowed room together. The tension had been building all evening, tiny notch by notch. She'd expected it, welcomed it, unfamiliar though it was. It was exciting. And yet now, here, there was this feeling that she had walked into another universe where she couldn't be sure of anything anymore. Not Jonas. Not herself. Least of all herself.

Then he started to undo her shirt, kissing the exposed flesh button by discarded button. And she remembered the scent of his hair, the taste of his skin, and that she knew his heartbeat. The universe flipped back to normal.

* * *

It seemed almost at once there was sunlight streaming through Hope's window, and she was waking up to the sound of a man looking for his shoes.

'Huh?' she said, swimming reluctantly up to consciousness.

'Good morning.'

That brought her awake fast. She shot upright on the pillows, realized she was naked and slid down again, holding the sheet to her breast in what she hoped was a casual manner. Though it was ridiculous after what they had done last night. But that was in the dark, and now the spring sun was insolently bright on the devastation of last night's activities.

There was a pillow lying on top of the dressing table. Remembering the circumstances in which she had kicked it to the ceiling, Hope blushed. Jonas followed her eyes and grinned. He flipped it up and tossed it over to her. She stuffed the pillow behind her. One-handed, of course, while she retained what she hoped looked like a firm but nonchalant grip on the covers.

'Th-thank you.'

The bed creaked as he sat on the side and bent to give her a quick, casual kiss. As if they had woken up together before, hundreds of times instead of just twice. 'How you feeling?'

'Not really awake yet.' It was even the truth.

'Wish I could stick around and wake you up properly. But it's tree-lopping day down in the forest.'

He kissed her again more lingeringly. He was clearly a morning person. Hope relaxed her convulsive grip on the covers and one hand slid round his shoulders.

'I can't,' he said thickly after a prolonged and pleasant interval. 'It's an early start. I promised Klaus.'

'Oh, I'm sorry.' She let go at once.

'Yeah, so am I.' He released her much more slowly and only after another long kiss. As if he were committing it to memory, thought Hope. She was amused but deeply touched too. She stopped caring that she was naked and swung her legs out of bed.

'I'll make you coffee at least.'

But he stood up, shaking his head. 'No time. Gotta go.'

But he didn't. Instead he gathered her to him and wasted several more minutes when he could have been on the road. Hope decided that being naked was a positive pleasure when you were in a full-body lock with a man who had all his clothes on and wished he hadn't. It felt deliciously decadent. She wondered why she hadn't thought of it before.

'Don't tempt me.'

She opened her eyes wide. 'Who's tempting? Look, I'm not even touching you.' And she took her arms away and waved them in the air teasingly.

He groaned as if he were really in pain. She beamed. He released her. 'I'm going. If I don't, you'll eat my soul and I will lose my reputation as the most obsessive volunteer on the books.'

Hope could not stop smiling. She could feel it from her eyebrows to her toenails. 'Poor lamb,' she crooned.

'I've never been late for a working party call in my life. Oh the hell with it . . . ' And he reached for her.

But she sidestepped neatly. 'I could never come between a man and his responsibilities,' she said primly. 'On your way, hot shot.'

He laughed. And went.

Hope shrugged herself into the glamorous garment on the back of the door: a black velvet full-skirted robe — thank you, Mrs Anton, stuffed her feet into flip-flops, and pattered after him. She caught him up on the stairs.

He raised an eyebrow, but he was already into man-going-to-work mode, with his jacket slung over one shoulder and the car keys in his hand. 'I wasn't joking. I really don't have time for coffee.'

'I know. But you may not be able to get out of the house without me. Did you see where I put the kitchen door key last night? It's a blank. Mind you, I'm quite proud that I remembered to lock up last night at all, given the distractions.'

His eyes gleamed. 'Impressive.'

He clearly remembered the distractions as well as she did. It was incredibly sexy. Hope gave a small voluptuous shiver and his eyes darkened.

'I focus well,' she said sedately.

Jonas folded his fingers round hers. They went down the rest of the staircase hand in hand.

Hope led the way to the kitchen. The key wasn't on its proper hook in the secret cupboard, but Jonas found where it had fallen and handed it to her. Hope gave a big sigh of relief and unlocked.

Jonas drew back the big bolts and opened the door onto a bright, cold day. He turned to say goodbye.

But Hope shook her head and knotted the tie of her robe tighter. 'I'll come and see you off.'

She walked with him to his car and stood watching, while he threw the jacket into the back. There was a film of moisture over the car, completely obscuring the windows. She found a tissue in the pocket of her robe and started to clean a wing mirror absently.

He took the tissue away from her. 'I'll do that. Don't get cold.'

'No, I won't.' She didn't move.

He took her hand and swung it gently.

'I'll call you.'

'Yes.'

Hope looked at his mouth. God, he was gorgeous.

He said raggedly, 'Don't do that.'

She jumped and flushed scarlet. His fingers tightened.

'Look, I've got to go and help the

guys make the site of that fallen tree safe. I'm committed, God help me. And you need to get some clothes on.'

Hope stood very still. It was so cold that the garden was white with spring frost. The breeze was icy. Yet for a moment all she wanted was for him to push her back against the cold, wet car and have her now. Just the thought of it made her gasp.

It seemed he was reading her mind. His eyes flared. 'You're not serious?'

She fell back against the car. The wind caught the skirt of her robe and wrapped it round Jonas's legs. The velvet tie slipped. She was trembling with cold and lust. She tugged on his hand, just a little.

For a heartbeat he resisted. Then, like a mountain tumbling, he crushed her against him. His mouth was hard on hers and his hands everywhere.

Hope caught fire. She fumbled for his zip. Her hands were shaking. She found he was as aroused as she was and heard him catch his breath. It seemed more than she could bear. Fiercely she clenched her body against him, one leg round his waist, as she reached to guide him into her. The velvet tie finally gave way and the robe billowed. She hardly noticed. They drove into each other, wordless. Her blood thundered in her ears. I must, I must . . . Her spine arched, her throat arched, the pleasure was almost anguish . . . And then she crested the peak and was soaring on a great cry of triumph.

Moments later he groaned and shuddered, like a glacier shaking itself free, and stumbled forward. He threw out one hand to brace himself against the car to stop himself crushing her and buried his face in her hair. They were both breathing hard.

For a long minute they stood where they were, both of them coming back to their senses, while the wind whipped her robe around them like a live thing. Then he took a steadying breath and shifted. Hope felt his lips move at her temple, where the pulse beat. Shaken, she put up a hand to touch his hair. It felt crisp — and damp.

'I — er — I think it's raining,' she said in a small voice.

Reluctantly, it seemed, Jonas raised his head and looked up. His chest was still rising and falling like a runner's. A fine rain, not much more than mist, had closed in. He gave a choke of laughter.

'Rain? More like thunderbolts and lightning. You know we're crazy, right?'

He put the back of his hand against her cheek. It was somehow more intimate than a kiss. She hugged him.

But he was already looking at his watch. 'And we need to start motoring.'

'You're going?'

'We're both wet, you're cold and I'm late. Of course I'm going. You need to get warm.'

He started to pull her robe together across her breasts to reinforce the point. But he was momentarily distracted and bent to drop a light kiss on her cold flesh before knotting the velvet tie tight again. Actually, not that light a kiss.

Hope jumped at the heat of it.

'Enough,' he said and she didn't know whether he was talking to her or himself. 'I'm going. I'll call you as soon as I can.'

He got into the car and drove off.

Hope watched him out of sight. She was shaking convulsively, while the robe and her hair tossed in the wind. She didn't notice. She couldn't believe what she had just done.

When the sound of the engine died in the mist, she turned and shot back into the house. It was nearly as cold as the outdoors. Her hands were clumsy on the lock and, when she looked, she saw that her fingers had gone white and were now turning blue at the ends.

'Bath,' she said, hugging herself. 'I'm a new woman!'

7

Jonas made it back to the rangers' centre in time to shower and change into clothes he hadn't been wearing yesterday. The Antons' car was still outside, of course. Nobody was tactless enough to comment.

He brimmed over with energy throughout the tree-felling expedition, carrying tools, heaving fallen branches off the tracks and wading into the stream to clear the beginnings of a fair dam. He even volunteered to stay behind and hammer all the waist-high DANGER signposts around the perimeter of the landslip. But Klaus said that he should do his share and no more.

'Fair enough,' said Jonas, leaping out of the stream and striding off to the vehicles to fetch hammers. He whistled all the way there and back.

Klaus raised his eyebrows. 'Having a

good holiday, then?'

'The best,' said Jonas with enthusiasm.

Back at the centre he called Hope. 'Hi. I'm back. How are you doing?'

'Feeling newly minted, to be honest.'

Jonas felt as if his face was one huge smile. 'Me too.'

She gave a little gasp.

If he closed his eyes he could see her expression. Witch-green eyes wide with surprise. Face soft. Lips parted. Desire hit him so hard that for a moment he couldn't speak. He heard her swallow and knew she was feeling the same. Speak? He could barely breathe for a moment.

Hope pulled herself together before he did. 'I've got to come and collect the car.'

He took control of his breathing. 'I'll bring it over.'

'You're not on the insurance policy.'

'Doesn't matter. I'm insured to drive anything but a tank.'

But she was still uneasy. 'It's my responsibility.'

'OK. I'll come and collect you and bring you back here, then.'

She demurred. Someone ran a taxi service in the village. The Antons had left her his number as a precaution. She could get a cab.

He laughed aloud. 'No need. I'm due a lunch break after a morning's manual labour.'

When consulted, Klaus agreed. 'And you can go shopping while you're at it. The energy bars are down to nothing after those boys got at them. Better change first though.'

Jonas was impatient to get going. 'Why?'

The chief ranger was brutal. 'You smell of rotting undergrowth and you look like a tramp.'

Jonas laughed and followed his advice.

Hope was waiting. Before he had cut the engine, she was out of the kitchen door and running towards him. He jumped out of the vehicle, opened his arms and swept her off her feet. She laughed as he swung her round crazily. And then she stopped laughing and they kissed for a long time.

When at last he let her go they stood there, smiling into each other's eyes.

'Now that's what I call a homecoming. I could get used to this.'

'Had a hard day at the office, dear?' she teased.

'I should say so. Chopping and sawing and putting up notices.'

'I'm impressed.' She meant it.

'I could show you my bruises,' he offered hopefully.

Hope shook her head, her whole body alight with their shared laughter. 'Good try, but the day isn't over yet. Maybe after I've repossessed the Antons' car and Moby has had his exercise.'

★   ★   ★

The days that followed fell into a pattern. Jonas would leave early on volunteer ranger duties. Hope linked up with Poppy for the morning ritual dog game, did necessary chores, and then followed him to the centre later. They spent the afternoons in the forest, or walking on the lower slopes of the mountains, skirting farms and vineyards, accompanied by an ecstatic Moby. In the evening, Jonas came home to her. They held hands a lot.

It felt as if they were in a magic bubble, he thought. He'd never felt so happy, so *right*. OK, there were things he hadn't told her yet. But these days were special. There would be plenty of time to let the outside world in later.

She cooked for him, disastrously, when she misread the recipe and added a tablespoonful of chilli powder to a casserole requiring a teaspoonful. Jonas rescued the dish by removing a quarter of the mixture and adding vast amounts of vegetables to that quarter. He took over the cooking.

In the tree-lopping, he tore a great triangle out of the sleeve of one of his shirts. Hope mended it with needle and thread from her travelling mending kit. He surveyed the neat, tiny stitches with astonishment. 'That's amazing.'

She smiled, pleased. 'When you travel light, a good mending kit is the best luxury.'

She told him about her travels, learning skills, learning languages, always moving on. He told her about his time as a student, both in England and the States, learning stuff he'd never expected to.

'My roommate was a musician. It was a crash course in music, just living in the same space. He took everything seriously, from monks singing plain chant to country.'

'Sounds nice.' She seemed almost wistful.

He flicked up an eyebrow. 'No roommates?'

'Not so much. Of course, accommodation often came with the job. Anyway, I liked my own space. I'd lived in a village where everyone knew everyone else's business all my life. It was great not to feel crowded.'

That worried him. 'Are you feeling crowded now, then?'

'In all this forest?' She danced round him, like Moby. 'Never.'

Jonas hugged her, relieved. Mostly relieved.

Hope had enchanted him from the moment he set eyes on her. Now he found that the more he knew her, the deeper he was falling in love. Falling in love like this had consequences. So his first instincts had been right. But what about Hope's instincts?

Sometimes he was certain she felt the same. But sometimes he just didn't know.

Carlo called him. Would he come back to the office, just for a day, well, a single meeting? The Very Difficult Client was passing through Liburno again and he really wanted to talk to Jonas.

Jonas agreed. Of course he did. But he felt the cold breath of the outside world on the back of his neck. Time was running out.

'Come with me,' he urged Hope.

She knew he was a lawyer, he reasoned. She could absorb the additional trivia of royalty while talking to his lawyer brothers. It was the ideal transition.

Only Hope wouldn't co-operate. 'What about Moby?'

'We'll leave him with Marko again.'

'Last time we had no choice. It was an emergency. This would be just so I could jaunt off to the city.'

'So?'

She nearly lost her temper. 'So this is my *job*. I'm *paid* to look after Moby. It's only for four weeks, for heaven's sake. You can wait another few days to show me the sights of Liburno.'

And that was another, stronger waft of the outside world. Not so much a breath as a full-on gale.

'But I want you with me,' he insisted.

They argued.

She really did lose her temper, then and slammed the kitchen door after him when he left.

Moby crept out from under the kitchen table when Jonas had gone. He looked so miserable that Hope sank down onto the tiled floor and put her arms round him. She pulled his ears gently, the way he liked, and he pushed his nose under her arm, with little grumbling noises of distress.

'Oh, Moby,' she said. 'Don't worry. I wouldn't leave you, no matter what the silly man said.'

But when she got up and tried to start clearing up the breakfast things, he followed her, shoving his whole head against her and looking at her worriedly until she started to pet him again. She hadn't seen him so upset since he went looking for Poppy in the forest. His whiskery eyebrows made him look worried.

'Maybe you don't like loud voices,' she said, rubbing the soft velvety cap at the top of his head. 'Nor do I.'

She remembered the shouting at home those last few months before her father was arrested. He'd been like Jonas was this morning: wilful, stubborn, determined to have his own way, utterly refusing to acknowledge that anybody had a higher duty than to himself and his interests. She'd got used to it from her father, in those terrible months, but it had repelled her, almost frightened her, to see it in someone else. Especially Jonas. He'd always seemed so reasonable until then.

Maybe she didn't know him as well as she thought she did.

Or maybe it had something to do with how soon she would be leaving. She was increasingly aware of how short a time they had left. Jonas must be the same. Maybe he was worried that she'd try to cling past her sell-by date. Hope winced at the thought.

There had been a guy like that in Australia — happy enough to swim and surf with her while the summer lasted but seriously worried when she made no plans to move on at the end of the season. 'We have to talk,' he'd said as they closed up the bar one night. 'You're a great girl, Hope. But I travel alone.'

'So do I,' she'd said smartly, and booked her flight out the next day.

She hadn't been expecting their summer fling to last any longer than he had, but it had been a nasty slap in the face all the same. Even half a thought that Jonas might be contemplating something similar made her feel sick.

* ★ ★

Jonas drove recklessly. He made the short journey to the city in record time and was in the office, showered, shaved, hair newly cut and in his lawyer suit early enough to read the relevant briefing papers twice over. The client was in a mood, so it was just as well.

The meeting went on very late. Jonas texted Hope to warn her. She didn't reply.

'Thank you for doing this,' said Carlo. 'I know it was a real pain. How is your — er — ?'

'My *er* is not so good, just at this moment.'

'Then I'm even more sorry,' said Carlo with genuine concern. 'Look, why don't you bring her to the vintage ball as consolation for missing your evening tonight?'

Jonas snorted. 'Because she'd loathe it. She says she hates dances and she's never wearing a ball gown again.' He remembered a little too clearly the shake in her voice as she told him.

Carlo blinked, clearly recognizing a direct quote. He flung up his hands. 'Right. Wouldn't work then. Sorry. I'll get back in my box.'

There was still no text from Hope. So Jonas went back to his Liburno apartment. He wouldn't have got to the Antons' villa before midnight, anyway, he reasoned. But it was really Hope's silence that kept him in the city.

He wandered round his own rooms and they felt strange. He had always liked living alone. It was partly why he had always refused an apartment in the castle, ever since he came of age. But now he felt — not lonely exactly. But as if something important was missing. Not a peaceful night.

The next morning he received a sober text from Hope: *Sorry I lost my rag.*

He replied: *Me too.*

And, as simply as that, what had been missing came back. Jonas couldn't believe it. He brewed coffee and tried to make sense of it. How could he possibly miss Hope in a place she'd never even been to? And then he realized: he missed not feeling at ease with her. He had got used to sharing his thoughts with her; teasing her and being teased; laughing at the same things; and arguing when she brought a completely new perspective to something he thought he already knew inside out.

Yet that stiff little text message was not what he wanted. Looking at it logically, it could have been from a stranger. A wisp of the former loneliness touched him again.

'No,' he almost shouted.

They belonged together. He knew it, bone-deep. He'd known it for ages. It had crystallized when they worked as a team to rescue the boy in the forest. But he'd known before that, really. And the feeling of rightness had just grown and grown over the last weeks.

He'd never felt anything like that before. But hadn't Jack said something like that when he got together with Celina? It had seemed unreal to Jonas back then. Now he thought maybe he could understand it.

He wondered whether Hope knew how he felt. Whether she felt the same. He thought she did, but he didn't understand their fight this morning. It seemed just to have blown up out of nowhere.

He tried to call her. But she wasn't picking up. Maybe she was driving. Or taking Moby for his walk out of reception range. Frustrated, he bashed out a text.

Taking you out for dinner. Let's drop off Moby on Marko again. We need to talk.

It wasn't perfect. But at least it signalled that this was important.

It wasn't until he was in the car, heading back for the villa, that Jonas remembered all the things he hadn't told her yet. It sent a chill through him. How on earth had he let it go on so long? He'd made that one decision, on the day they met, not to introduce himself as Prince Jonas of San Michele, and after that he'd just taken one day at a time. He'd enjoyed being plain volunteer ranger Reval. He'd even started to *think* like plain ranger Reval, for heaven's sake.

Driving back from Liburno, he faced it. For the last three weeks, he'd been living in a soap bubble. And all that time he'd been storing up a load of stuff to explain and never realized it. Well, it was too late to change that now. He'd just have to do the best he could. And hope she'd understand.

But somehow, as soon as they were together, all his plans fell apart. In fact, they both seemed to feel they were in uncharted territory tonight.

Maybe because he'd invited her out, she had dressed up a little. Oh, it was nothing grand, just different from what he was used to from Hope. She had put up her hair so that little tendrils caressed her neck distractingly. And she was wearing a jaunty white blazer and a silky scarf he hadn't seen before. The peacock colours made her eyes look very green. More witchy than woodland, he thought uneasily. And he had never seen her wear make-up before.

He'd thought it would be a good idea to free them up from the need to cook so they could talk. But even before they reached the restaurant, it wasn't working.

Hope seemed determined to make bright conversation. The evening began to develop all the awkwardness of a first date. She even handed Moby over to Marko with all the careful courtesy of a woman meeting the boyfriend's friends and family for the first time. Jonas began to feel as if he were drowning.

He kept trying to find an opening for everything he needed to say. But every time he started the subject, she deflected the conversation to Moby, Poppy, previous employers who had amused her, or where she might move on to next in her attempt to see the whole world. It was as if they'd become strangers overnight, he thought, appalled.

At last he put down his knife and fork and said, 'Stop. Just stop. Please.'

She went blank. 'What?'

'I need to talk to you. Properly.'

She flinched. 'Can't we just have a nice meal and chat about nothing much? I'll be gone soon.' She sounded almost desperate.

Jonas had reached his now-or-never point. 'Exactly. I don't want you to go.' Not very romantic, he noticed in passing, but it would have to do for the moment. 'But first I have to tell you — '

But Hope had sat bolt upright, an expression of outrage on her face. 'Is that why you've been sulking all evening?'

It was so unfair that he was moved to protest. 'I don't sulk. I've just got a lot on my mind.'

But she interrupted. 'That's *exactly* what my father used to say.' All the social manners fell away. She leaned forward, eyes blazing. 'Whenever he didn't get his own way. Whenever anyone challenged him. Even when the police came along with a cast-iron case that he'd been misleading investors for years and the lawyers told him to plead guilty. He just said, 'They misunderstood. I had a lot on my mind.'' The mimicry was savage.

Jonas stared, stunned.

'I hate it.' She was shaking her head so that the pins that had skewered her beautiful hair into place cascaded down her shoulders. One fell onto her trout with almonds. She didn't notice. 'The lies! The evasions! The ghastly refusal to accept responsibility!'

He couldn't entirely deny that, he thought ruefully. He said, 'I'm trying to be responsible now.'

''I don't want you to go'?'

It was Jonas's turn to wince. He'd known that was a mistake as soon as he said it, after all. 'I only meant that I need to clear up some things before I ask you . . .'

But she wasn't listening. 'I won't tolerate it. Never again. Not from anyone else. Not from *you*.'

Jonas looked at Hope's glittering eyes and realized with shock that she was on the point of tears. A real storm of tears, too. Hurriedly he fished out one of the laundered handkerchiefs that he'd stuffed into his pocket in the apartment and passed it across the table to her. She blotted her face, then blew her nose defiantly and sank back against the settle. There was a long silence.

She closed her eyes. 'I'm . . . sorry. I don't think that was about you.'

'I know.'

He reached across the table to take her hand, but she shot backwards. Not looking at him, she mopped her eyes some more and sipped her water.

Jonas wanted desperately to take her into his arms. She looked so unhappy — spiky, exhausted, and untouchable.

His heart bled for her. But there wasn't one thing he could do. This was her private struggle. Her whole body was shouting it. She drank more water, clearly deep in unhappy memories. He waited.

'I suppose I've been bottling all that up for years,' she said at last in a small voice. 'I was so *angry* with him. Only, he was so bewildered. And then he got ill.' Her voice ran out. Her eyes filled again. 'It would have been like kicking an old dog who couldn't move,' she said bleakly. She swallowed.

Jonas took a policy decision. He didn't think either of them was going to eat any more; and whatever happened next, he was sure it needed to take place on their own. He signalled for the bill. 'Let's go.'

She didn't say anything in the car. But when they got back to the villa she said, 'Could we walk a little?' Jonas nodded.

The moon was nearly full and very bright. He took her hand and she

squeezed his fingers in silent acknowl-
edgement. They walked down the lane a
little and stood on the old bridge over
the river, looking across the fold of
valley and hills where the vines were
invisible in the night. She shivered.

He took off his jacket and settled it
round her shoulders over the pretty
linen blazer. The tension seemed to leak
out of Hope as they stood there in
silence.

Eventually she leaned against his
shoulder. The night breeze caught her
descending hair and blew strands across
her face and his.

'I should have a headscarf like that
lady in the post office.' He could hear
the smile in her voice.

'All right now?'

Her hair moved against his cheek as
she nodded.

'Then shall we go home?'

Jonas was more than half expecting
her to say that she wanted to be alone.
But Hope turned and kissed him hard
and then said, 'Yes. Oh yes. Please.'

They made love with tenderness. With passion. Even, sometime in the small hours, with laughter again. But above all, with total honesty. She could not have told him she trusted him any more clearly.

Humbled and profoundly grateful, Jonas thought, *Now I know she feels the same as I do. We can work this out now. In the morning.*

* * *

But in the morning the world intruded with a vengeance. Mrs Anton called with the news that Poppy had broken her arm and was being airlifted back to Liburno for treatment.

'And all she wants is to be with Moby. Could you possibly bring him to meet us?' Mrs Anton began to cry.

'Poor Poppy,' said Hope in quick sympathy. 'Poor you. Of course.'

'I'll drive you,' said Jonas.

But his cell phone was already beeping. 'Have you got a moment?' said

Carlo, sounding strained.

The Difficult Client had stormed back into the office, even more vitriolic than normal, with a major commercial dispute that had blown up overnight. He was now threatening to take it to every international court he could think of. Carlo didn't actually order Jonas back to the office, but when he said, 'We're really missing you,' Jonas grimaced.

'Time's run out on us, sweetheart,' he said to Hope. And to Carlo: 'I'll be there as soon as I can.' Then to Hope: 'Did I sound as grudging as I feel?'

She shook her head. 'Very supportive.'

'That's a relief. No one could have a better boss.'

'Then he deserves his great brother.'

'At least we'll both be in Liburno,' Jonas and Hope said in chorus. They laughed, and stood with their arms locked round each other, reluctant to say goodbye.

'I still need to talk to you,' Jonas said

between kisses. 'As soon as I've dealt with this latest crisis.'

'I'll keep my diary free,' she teased. 'Now go. Your brother needs you.'

'You're a hard woman.' But he disengaged and got into the car. 'I'll call you as soon as I'm out of the meeting.'

She watched him until his car was out of sight.

But Poppy had more than a broken arm. She had suspected concussion. She was certainly not making sense by the time Hope and Moby met them. Hope drove them straight to the clinic from the airport.

Mrs Anton was half-mad with worry and didn't want to let Hope out of her sight. 'Have you got another job to go to at the end of the week, Hope?'

'No.'

'Could you stay working for us?'

'Glad to.'

She texted Jonas.

They texted a lot over the next few days. Jonas went off on a rescue mission to the Difficult Client's lawyers in

London while Hope ran a ten-hour working day round Moby and the invalid. When the rest of the family returned from their trip, it went up to fourteen hours. Poppy was still in hospital, not responding as well as everyone had hoped.

Hope texted everything to Jonas as it happened. Sadly, she looked at the family's schedule and sent: *Can't see me getting away this week.*

He replied: *Of course you can't. I've got lots of boring work to keep me busy. Don't worry. Love you.*

And then Poppy had a relapse and Mrs Anton asked Hope for another favour. It was a lot tougher.

'Blake's got this official dinner tonight. We've taken a table and he needs a hostess. But I can't leave Poppy. I *can't*. Please help us out, Hope. There's no one else we could ask this late.'

Hope didn't try to hide how much she hated the idea. How she loathed big parties, had none of the right clothes, and generally would rather climb the Alps in her bare feet.

Blake Anton looked dreadful. 'My wife would be really grateful,' was all he said. But Hope could see how hard he was finding it to stay reasoned and courteous. He checked his phone every spare moment he had — and some that clearly weren't spare.

'Oh what the hell,' she said. 'It's only one evening out of my life. I can stand it, if you can.'

She texted Jonas but wasn't surprised to get no reply. He'd said that he had some lawyer event that evening and would have his phone off. He must already have left.

So Hope dressed in a frenzy. Mrs Anton had directed her to borrow a sophisticated bronze satin dress that was a lot more figure-hugging than Hope normally wore. Fortunately she was slimmer than her employer. Mrs Anton had bought high-heeled strappy shoes to go with the gown, too. They were also too big. But with some party gel for tired feet and an extra hole drilled in the strap, they worked well enough. She put her hair up rapidly.

'It's the official declaration of last year's vintage. The wine buyers have been in town for two days. Tonight is to celebrate it. It's at San Michele's premier vineyard, hosted by the royal family,' Blake Anton explained, whipping through his text messages. 'Our guests — '

'I know who the guests are. Mrs Anton gave me the list with bios attached. I've learned what I can and it's on my phone if I forget anything.'

For a moment his mood lightened. 'You're a miracle.'

She chuckled. 'You won't say that when I fall off these shoes.'

But she concentrated hard and it seemed all right. She had to remind herself to stop fiddling with the feathery curls against her neck and to keep the matching silk shawl over her bare shoulders in case the too-large dress slipped too far. But apart from that she felt altogether more relaxed than she would have dreamed possible.

I must remember to tell Jonas, she thought. *He may just have cured me of my party phobia.*

The chateau was a jewel, set in breath-taking formal gardens full of neatly trimmed hedges, life-size sculptures and one of the largest baroque fountains she had ever seen. They entered through wide double doors into a vestibule with a marble floor, massive portraits and chaises longues against each wall. A great curving staircase led to what the attendants described as the anteroom.

A flunky told them, 'San Michele wine is being served. The royal party will join you there.'

Hope remembered the first time she had drunk San Michele wine. She smiled and blushed a little, hugging the memory. Something else to tell Jonas. It would make him laugh.

The anteroom seemed to stretch the entire width of the house. It was full to bursting point with chattering people in their best, the men in tuxedos or impressive military uniforms with braids and medals, the women in ball gowns and jewels.

The royal party arrived without a fanfare. Someone pointed out Crown Princess Anna, circulating graciously a few feet away. In the middle of the room, she met up with her husband, and they headed up what rapidly turned into a column of special guests shuffling in line to go to the top table.

'It's like primary school,' Hope said involuntarily. 'We used to go to the swimming baths in a crocodile like that when I was eight.'

One of Blake Anton's guests said, 'You know, you're right.'

And Hope thought that maybe she might actually enjoy this party after all, in spite of the ball gowns.

She must tell Ally Parker as well as Jonas. Ally and she had always walked together to the swimming class. These days Ally was an interviewer for

Celebrity magazine and presumably knew all about grand parties. But she might not have come across the royalty crocodile protocol. It would make her laugh.

The crown princess led the way into the banqueting hall on the arm of a tall distinguished-looking man with white hair, a sash and medals.

'Guest of honour,' someone murmured. 'Master sommelier. The lady with Prince Carlo is head of the San Michele winemakers' association.'

There followed a procession to the long top table with everyone else falling in behind. Blake Anton, who did big formal dinners all the time, had consulted the seating plan well in advance and efficiently located his own table. It was in front of some magnificent gold and glass doors.

Hope, seated between an American master of wine and a French wine writer, realized it was going to be a long evening. Train spotters, she thought, would be thrilling by comparison. But she smiled and listened to them both in turn, and tried to look as if wine fascinated her as much as it did them.

'Don't worry.' The American was proving much more down-to-earth than his French colleague. 'The big speeches were all done this afternoon at the tasting. Someone will thank the crown princess. She will thank us all for coming. And then the dancing starts.'

'I look forward to it,' she said courteously. It was true. After two hours of acidity, malolactic fermentation and noble rot, dancing, even in these shoes, would be a welcome relief.

★ ★ ★

His Serene Highness Prince Jonas was wearing the formal mess dress uniform of a commander of the Royal San Michele Navy. It was, as he said himself, a snazzy number in navy-blue with gold buttons and epaulettes, aiguillettes, a white waistcoat and a black bow tie. No one could call him unobtrusive. But he was, at least, sword-free.

He was also, now, in a towering temper. He'd received a text that made him roar like a hunting lion, after which the palace staff, who were used to him as the amenable brother, walked round him on tiptoe.

Jonas knew it and was powerless to hide his fury. It was so *unfair*. The woman hated dances. She said so herself. She had no right to change her mind at absolutely the worst moment.

All those times when he had so nearly told her the full truth about himself, and decided not to because the time hadn't felt right! Well no time could be worse than now. And now he had no choice but to tell her. In fact he'd be lucky if he got to tell her himself before some busybody said, 'Oh look, there's Prince Jonas.'

He'd called for a guest list. Any faint hope that Blake Anton was taking his guests to some other celebration faded at the first glance. The list was alphabetical. The Antons were at the top. There was even a note beside Mrs Anton's name that she would be absent and represented by Miss Hope Kennard, due to Poppy Anton (aged eleven) being in hospital with complications following concussion. The crown princess was advised to say a few words of sympathy to Mr Anton. His party was at Table 8.

Jonas consulted a floor plan. Table 8 was by the windows onto the terrace. That might help. But he'd have to work fast.

'I need someone to deliver a note,' he barked. '*Now.*'

* * *

Hope decided that big parties weren't so bad after all. She had danced a sedate waltz with the French wine writer and a distinctly more adventurous polka with a San Michele viniculturist. The crown princess had visited their table, offering Blake Anton her sympathy and wishing all the foreigners welcome to San Michele. And then a footman cleared his throat behind Hope and slid a note onto the table in front of her.

'To reach the statue garden you go out of these doors, turn left, and then left again onto the west terrace,' he murmured.

'Er, thank you. I think.'

She looked round. But no one had noticed her note arriving. Half her fellow guests were dancing and the rest were chatting either to someone else at the table or somewhere in the room.

She opened it. The signature was almost illegible. But then her eyes adjusted to the rapid scrawl and the reception became the best party she'd ever been to.

Darling, I'm here too. Work, of course. I've got a load of duty dances. I'll be in the statue garden 10.15 — 10.45. Meet me there, if you can.

There was a big black arrow, telling her to turn over. On the other side he had scrawled a truly appalling map. Just as well that the footman had told her how to get there, she thought.

She picked up her bag and shawl, smiled generally round the table and slipped out onto the terrace into the crisp evening air. Someone had put pyramid heaters on the terrace, living flame in a glass case, and people were grouped close to them, laughing and drinking, several of them smoking. They took no notice as she strolled past them.

Once she came to the very end of the terrace and rounded the corner, it was like being in a different world. It was cold without the warmth from the ballroom or the pyramid heaters. The far garden was in darkness, but Hope saw statues illuminated by chilly blue spotlights. The fountain, too. It was a bit creepy, if she were honest. She didn't care. Jonas was out there somewhere.

She ran down the terrace, completely forgetting that she didn't trust Mrs Anton's shoes. Her feet barely touched the ground.

Shallow steps curved down into the

statue garden, faintly lit by small inset spots. Someone was standing there in the half-dark. She knew the set of his shoulders, the tilt of his head; the way he moved the moment he heard her footsteps.

She stopped. 'Jonas.' It was a whisper of joy, of excitement. Of homecoming.

'Hope? *Hope?*'

He took the last steps three at a time and caught her up in his arms. 'My darling, my darling. I thought I'd missed you. Kiss me.'

He sounded so shaken that she almost didn't recognize his voice. But she recognized the way he held her, one hand spread between her shoulder blades, the other thumb stroking her jawline convulsively, as if he couldn't believe she was there. She laughed softly, as she had done before, and feathered a kiss across the stroking palm.

Jonas gave a choking laugh. So he remembered too. 'Tease. Not like that.'

His arms tightened and she gave

herself into that wondrously familiar full-body kiss, all her senses on fire. She cried out in a kind of anguish and he broke the kiss, holding her strongly while they got their breathing under control.

'You smell different,' she said lovingly, when she could speak.

'Do I?' The boa constrictor grip might have lessened, but he wasn't letting her go any time soon. He pretended to sniff her neck experimentally and ended by kissing her throat. 'You don't.'

Her head tipped back under his exploring mouth but she said a little breathlessly, 'Not very complimentary. I must have smelled of rainwear and wet dog mostly.'

'Nope.' Then he found her mouth again, and breathing was no longer a possibility.

Later, when they were sitting on the top step leaning against each other, she said, 'You usually smell of the forest.'

He was startled. 'Do I?'

'And now it's something very indoors-y and sophisticated.'

'*Sophisticated!*' He hooted. 'Probably mothballs.'

She reared away from him, half-laughing, half genuinely astonished. 'What?'

'Damn uniform. It only gets an outing a couple of times a year. I always have to dress up in some uniform or other for these damn things. I don't know why. My father never does. But my sister-in-law has this bee in her bonnet . . .'

'But why?' she said. 'I'm sure it's very smart. But why wear it if you don't like it?'

'Ah.'

For some reason she thought, *That doesn't sound good.* 'What's wrong?'

'Nothing.'

Hope tried humour. 'I'm sorry to tell you this, Jonas, but you're a terrible liar. You're not even trying to sound convincing.'

It didn't work. He said stiffly, 'I'm sorry about that.'

217

She had never heard him sound like that before. It almost scared her. She refused to give in to it and tried to make a joke instead. 'There's no need to sound like a customs officer about to make me open my bags.'

'Oh God!'

'I'm sorry?' Hope said blankly.

And then suddenly there was a light at the end of the balustrade. Someone was swinging a small lantern. A voice hissed, 'Your Serene Highness? Are you there?'

Instinctively they both huddled down, out of sight. Grateful for the lightening of the atmosphere, Hope laughed silently and whispered, 'They must have lost a royal!'

He didn't laugh with her. Maybe that was when she knew something was badly wrong. Or maybe she was still trying to tell herself that her dawning suspicions were all down to her own wretched imagination.

Either way, Jonas went very still. And then he said in a heavy voice that she really didn't recognize, 'No they haven't lost anyone. Stay here. Or you'll really hate the fuss that will break out.'

And, just like that, between one second and the next, her suspicions crystallized, were justified and brought her world crashing round her ears.

Jonas stood up and went along the narrow terrace to meet the man with the lantern.

Crouching in the darkness on the steps, Hope heard him say in his own language, 'I'm just coming.'

'Message from Count Fredrik, Sir. The mayor of Liburno is the next on your dance card. She sat out her dance with the head of the growers' association, and now she's in a terrible temper. Count Fredrik says please can you can reconcile the warring parties?'

Hope was numb. *At least I'm getting better at the language*, she thought with something between righteous fury and despair.

'Go back to Count Fredrik and tell him I'll be right there.'

Your Serene Highness. Count Fredrik. The mayor of Liburno. Reconcile the warring parties.

Hope took off her shoes, so they shouldn't give her away clippetty-clopping on the stone staircase, and slipped — no, *ran* — into the darkness of the garden.

At least I can't get lost. Turn left at one of those blasted statues and I'll find the main drive. And where there's a drive, there's a gate to leave by. Eventually.

Behind her she thought she heard Jonas call, 'Hope? Hope? Where are you?'

But she could have been wrong. Anyway, she couldn't face him.

His Serene Highness. Oh he was serene all right. Telling her bare-faced lie after lie! Getting his fellow rangers to cover for him! For they all had to know, didn't they? Probably those Boy Scouts at the rescue knew too. Now she came to think about it, one of them even called him *principe*, didn't he?

And she'd wondered vaguely if the word meant a winch! And even before that, when the head-scarfed lady had curtseyed to him, Hope had written it off as a quaint local custom.

How could I have been so stupid?

She heard the sound of running feet behind her and broke into a sprint. She was *not* going to be caught and questioned by security. She was *not* going to admit she even knew their damn Serene Highness, damn his lying eyes.

Only, of course, it wasn't security. And, also of course, he knew the chateau grounds too well. She pelted round a ten-foot box tree, topiarized to within an inch of its unfortunate life, and ran straight into a familiar chest.

'Oof,' she said, recoiling.

Jonas steadied her by her elbows. Her shoes flew out of her hand. Neither of them noticed. He was carrying the lantern that had nearly discovered her and was breathing hard.

'I need to talk to you.'

'Bit late for that.' Hope was shaking so hard, she could have been at the north pole. Dammit, even her teeth were chattering.

He said in his reasonable, I-know-I-can-make-you-agree-with-me voice, 'I know. I messed up. I've been trying to tell you but things kept getting in the way. I wanted to take time to do it properly, explain, find the right moment. I'm sorry.'

'You *lied* to me.' Even to herself, she sounded as if her vocal cords were coated in ice. Well it was better than weeping and shouting and trying to claw his eyes out. Wasn't it?

'Actually, I didn't lie, you know. I always told you my real name.'

Hope huddled her arms round herself. God, she was cold. Right through to her bones. She felt as if she'd walked under that forest waterfall and found that the water was straight off the snowfields. The sensation of melting ice cascading down her spine just went on and on.

'My father used to say things like that,' she said remotely. ''I didn't lie. I just left bits out. They could have found everything out if they'd bothered to check.' He believed it. Do you?'

Jonas flinched. 'Ouch.'

'Odd, isn't it? With my family history, you'd think I'd check everything that anyone tells me. I do, most of the time. How odd that I should have decided to trust you.' Her words bit.

'It wasn't like that.'

She made a dismissive gesture. 'Whatever.'

'Hope, listen to me.'

'Take your hands off me.'

He started to swear, and bit it off with an almost visible attempt at self-control. 'I never meant to deceive you.'

She laughed. It was a horrible grating noise.

Jonas began to sound alarmed. 'Look, I've got to . . . '

' . . . go and dance with the mayor of Liburno. I know. Off you go.'

He pushed a distracted hand through his hair. 'Yes. OK. I do have to. But we can talk afterwards.'

She backed away, barefooted on the cold grass, staring at him in the lantern light as if she had never seen him before. She nearly tumbled over one of her discarded shoes. She scooped it up and, with the accuracy of concentrated fury, launched it at a statue of a droopy-looking lady in dangerously loose draperies. The impact echoed round the silent garden.

'Hope, for heaven's sake,' he said, half-laughing, all charm and negotiating skills. 'Just come back with me.'

Hope really hated him then. 'So you can smarm me into saying it's OK? It's not OK.'

He took her by the shoulders. She went rigid.

'Look, we can work this out. I'm sorry there was a misunderstanding . . . '

'No misunderstanding,' said Hope icily. 'You lied. The end.' She felt turned to stone by his deceit. She stepped back and his arms fell. He seemed bemused. 'We are so over,' she said. 'And just in case you were thinking of it — don't contact me again.'

8

Hope decided to go home to Combe St Philip.

It was a first. Ever since she was eighteen, whenever she had setbacks or problems, she sorted them out herself. She never ran home to her brother.

She'd always reasoned that Max had more than enough on his plate, with an ex-wife who couldn't make up her mind whether she wanted to keep him on a string or not, and two small children he adored but didn't see enough. Not to mention an estate that Gerald Kennard had run to near-ruin and a house that had been in the family forever, with all the endless repairs that entailed.

But this time was different.

'I'm sorry,' she said to Mrs Anton. She tried to sound as if she was genuinely contrite, but the ice round her heart was a mile deep by then and it didn't really work. 'I can't take the job, after all. I need to go home.'

Mrs Anton didn't argue. She'd taken one look at Hope's face in the morning and been angelically incurious ever since. 'Whatever you want, my dear.'

Explaining to Poppy was harder. The little girl tried gallantly not to cry, but her lower lip quivered and she held tight to Moby. 'Will you come back when you've been home?'

Hope managed to say, 'I don't know,' and make it convincing.

The ice cracked a bit when she said goodbye to them. Girl and dog stood on the station platform, waving as long as she could see them and probably longer. Hope had to swallow hard and blow her nose several times before she could put that out of her mind.

Of Jonas, she tried not to think at all. There had been several calls to her cell phone from a number she didn't recognize. The resolution not to pick up was like a physical pain. But the memory of him saying, 'Actually, I didn't lie' hurt worse.

She'd thought she'd learned. She'd been proud of her instincts, her judgement. Again and again, she'd turned away from people because something had told her that she couldn't trust them. That even if they didn't exactly lie, they left out the really important things. She had been so sure . . .

And then Jonas Reval had called her a dryad, and she'd just thrown it all away. She hardly noticed the gaps in what he'd told her about himself. She laid out her history for him, like a map. But he hadn't told her anything about his home, his upbringing. Just stuff about his student days. And who knew how much of that was real? Cooking pasta for a bunch of musicians? Would a prince really do that? Or would he just say he did it to lull a stupid foreigner into having a four-week affair? Because he'd known exactly how long her job with the Antons would last. She'd told him herself.

Oh, he was good. Hope flayed herself with that thought. She was no better than a teenager with her first crush on a boy. All that experience, all that time travelling and meeting people and learning — wasted! And now she was right back where she'd started, weeping because love put a blindfold on you and left you to fall off a cliff.

No more weeping, she promised herself.

And then her own thoughts caught up with her. *Love put a blindfold on you.*

Love.

How had she never said that before? Not to Jonas. Not to herself. But it was true.

She loved him.

She knew it with absolute certainty. Now that it was over.

She leaned her head against the train window and let the tears seep out of her until she had none left.

Before she changed trains, she went to the ladies' room and splashed cool water on her face, especially her puffy eyelids. She even combed her hair. Then, on a rare whim, applied a little lipstick. By the time she saw her brother, she was going to be her own woman again.

And three days later she got out of the taxi that brought her from the station in the nearest market town.

'Drop me by the market cross,' she told the taxi driver. She didn't want him to drive her up to the front door. The last thing Max needed was for her to get the family all over the tabloids again. And there was a real chance that the paparazzi would still be interested that Hope Kennard, the fraudster's daughter, had come home to Hasebury Hall at last. The news would seep out eventually, of course it would, in a village like Combe St Philip. But Hope had every intention of being safely under cover in London by that time.

She said so to Max when she eventually tracked him down in one of the great glasshouses at the far end of the kitchen garden. He was repotting a forest of seedlings, grim with concentration, and didn't notice her approach at first. But when she said, 'Hello, Max,' he looked up and stared as if he couldn't believe his eyes.

'Hope?' He flung the trowel away from him and rushed to pick her up in a bear hug, muddy gardener's gloves and all. 'Oh, Hopey, it's good to see you.' And he swung her round until her feet left the ground, just as he used to when she was a child.

Hope began to laugh. And then she cried. He put her down and looked at her searchingly.

'Sorry,' she said, scrubbing the back of her hand across her eyes. 'Long journey.'

'Hmm. Coffee?'

He relieved her of her backpack, as he'd always done, and carried it ceremoniously up to the house, where he found some digestive biscuits and started to make coffee.

Hope sank bonelessly onto one of the

old chairs, looking round. The kitchen was bigger and emptier than she remembered, she thought. Of course, she was thinking of the big weekend parties her parents had held during the good times. The cook and her husband had been long gone before Hope actually left on her travels.

'How have you been?' they said simultaneously. And then laughed.

Hope made a gesture. 'You first.'

'Kids are fine. Ben likes his new form teacher. Holly's going to be a ballerina.'

Hope pulled a face. 'That'll be expensive.'

Max grinned down at her. 'I'm not worried. Last week she wanted to be a cavalier. That girl has a rich fantasy life.'

'And the business?'

'Surprisingly good. Landscape is a bit slow at this time of year, but the pot plants for offices project just keeps growing.'

'Good. You deserve it.' Hope knew how much it had hurt him, when he had to sell off land that had been in the family for generations to meet their father's debts, and how hard he had worked since to build a viable business to keep Hasebury Hall going. She tactfully didn't mention his ex-wife, who'd moved on to a man who earned more and worked fewer hours.

'And what about you?' Max put a mug of coffee in front of her and got milk from the fridge.

'Oh you know. Bit of this. Bit of that.' Was she trying too hard to sound bright? Hope wondered. 'I thought I'd come home and see spring this year. I love an English spring.'

'Oh to be in England, now that April's there?'

'Exactly,' she said, grateful.

'What about the kid you were looking after?'

Hope managed not to wince. 'She's fine. Her parents are back now and she's healing well.'

'And the forester guy?'

Hope was suddenly aware of a great big solid lump in her throat. She just shook her head, praying that her eyes wouldn't fill with tears.

Max didn't say anything.

'Anyway, I'm tired of living in backwaters. I want me some metropolitan buzz. I thought I'd try Aunt Cindy, see if she can find me a job with one of her smart mates.'

'London? Doesn't sound your scene.'

'Oh I don't know. I'll be a small fish in a bloody big pond.'

'Are you going into hiding, Hope?'

'I suppose I am,' she said on a note of discovery.

He looked worried, but bless him, he didn't criticize, much less argue. 'Well, if you must, you must. And London's certainly the place to do it. You can disappear like an eel in mud there.'

'Sounds perfect.' She meant it.

★ ★ ★

Aunt Cindy, when approached, offered enthusiastic help. Hope went to London.

Cindy Grace was no real relation, but

she and her husband had been regular attendees at the big parties at Hasebury Hall for a couple of years when Hope was small. Cindy's husband had died, about the time that Gerald Kennard was first arrested, and she had come to stay for a while. Then she had turned herself into a businesswoman and gone off to live in London.

Hope always felt that she had nothing to hide from Aunt Cindy, who had seen the Kennard family at their lowest point. Besides, she liked her. So she was taken aback by the style of her home — overstuffed cushions and objets d'art on every available surface weren't what she would have expected from the practical Mrs Grace, who had brought common sense and restored order to the distraught Kennard household.

She gave Hope tea in an ultra-feminine sitting room and grilled her gently in a manner worthy of an ambassador's widow. 'How long are you back for?'

Hope shrugged. 'How long is a piece of string?'

'No commitments elsewhere then?'

'No commitments,' Hope agreed steadily.

'Ah.' Cindy looked at her notes. 'You say you have no qualifications or particular skills but you're practical. Can you sew?'

Hope nodded.

'And you don't mind what you do? Have I got that right?'

Hope nodded again.

'Well then, I have a job for you, if you're interested.'

Hope felt a great rush of relief. It had been like holding her breath for too long, having no job, trying not to think about Jonas, not knowing where she was going to live. 'Oh, that's great. Who with?'

'Me.'

'What?' Hope was appalled. Cindy had changed beyond belief, it seemed. If she wanted some sort of assistant, surely she could see that Hope wasn't . . . well, girly or elegant enough? 'I mean it's very kind of you, but . . . '

Cindy looked amused. 'Do you even know what I do, Hope?'

'Um — no. Sorry.'

Cindy waved her apology away as of no importance. 'I plan weddings for people too busy, too fraught, or feeling too out of their depth to do it for themselves. We're just coming into our busiest season.'

'I'm not good enough at sewing to make a wedding dress,' said Hope, even more alarmed.

'Of course not. But it's an essential skill for running repairs.'

'Oh well then, I can do emergency mending all right.'

Cindy beamed. 'You could be a great asset. Though I'd like you to meet my assistant Natalya first. She's what I call the troubleshooter. I'm more of a big-picture person. She fixes things. You'd be working with her, if you come on board. But I think you'll get on. She's another one with a suspected broken heart.'

Hope froze.

Cindy gave her a bland smile and picked up the phone. 'Hi, Natalya. Would you join us, please?'

That was when Hope realized that the suffocatingly pretty rooms she'd seen so far must be a business space. She gave a great sigh of relief, especially when Natalya turned out to be a jeans-clad powerhouse with a friendly smile and absolutely no patience with romance.

'Basically, this business is event management with seriously loopy clients,' she said, showing Hope round the office downstairs when Cindy left them alone. 'No matter what they come up with, you have to take it seriously, cost it and sometimes point out how it affects their guests. After that, if they still want to go ahead, you do it, even if the mother-in-law will never speak to the bride again.' She thought for a moment. 'Unless it actually involves blood sacrifice, I suppose.'

Hope gave a snort of laughter. 'That bad?'

'And then some.' Natalya had a lovely smile, like a mischievous monkey. 'Fortunately, Cindy does all the diplomatic stuff. I'd just tell them to get real. But she says, 'Oh yes, a sub-aqua wedding would be lovely,' and then starts exploring issues like hair and photographs and how you get a tubby ninety-year-old aunt into a wetsuit. And they work it out for themselves. Mostly.'

'So what would you want me to do?'

'Support me. Do research I haven't time for. Pick up and deliver stuff, especially if it's urgent. Herd flower girls, under my direction. By the way, your weekends won't be your own from mid-May onwards. Is that a problem?'

'No.'

'Good. Welcome to the team.'

★ ★ ★

Jonas was working like a demon. He was in the office before it was light and often stayed until midnight. He worked through lunch. His work output was phenomenal. He took no personal phone calls and turned down all invitations, including semi-official ones from the palace.

'The rest of us are going to run out of cases if you go on like this,' joked his brother Carlo.

Jonas just nodded and went back into his office. And closed the door. Carlo gave up.

In the end, Jonas did what he always did. He went back to the forest. 'I'm going out,' he told his PA. 'Won't be back for the rest of the day.'

He avoided the rangers' centre and plunged straight into the trees. Eventually he stood still, listening for the sounds of small animals, the chatter of the stream nearby. He'd shared all those things with Hope. Would the waterfall still be carrying ice down from the mountains? Birds called whose names he'd learned as a boy in long walks with his godfather. He'd shared that with her too.

None of his family understood about

his feeling for the forest, but Hope did. She'd said he knew the forest soundscape as well as he knew his own heartbeat.

And then, in the scientists' hideout, what had she said? 'I can hear your heartbeat. I'd know it anywhere.'

Remembering, he felt again the astonishing tidal surge of feeling. *Shared* feeling. He would stake his life on it. They had been utterly together then. Totally open to each other. He hadn't even thought of telling her that he was prince then. It hadn't mattered.

He said it to himself again. It hadn't mattered. For the first time in years, it hadn't been a straitjacket. And that was because of Hope. She'd made his life bearable. No, more than that. She'd given him a glimpse of a way of being himself, at peace, not endlessly feeling as if he was limping along trying to please other people and not very good at it.

He thought, *I need her. I thought she needed me.* That night when she had stood beside him on the midnight bridge, slowly coming out of her dark place, holding his hand. That closeness, deeper than words.

Surely he hadn't been wrong about that?

They'd both known it. They'd acknowledged it that night in every way there was.

No matter what she said, she had *known*.

That was when he decided. He had to follow her. If she sent him away after he'd talked to her properly, so be it. But first he had to *try*.

9

The next problem for Hope was somewhere to live. She looked at a few websites and was making a shortlist, when she got an unexpected text.

Foreign junketings over then?

Ally!

Her heart lifted. Ally Parker was her very best friend. They'd gone to primary school together, and Ally had been Hope's mentor and protector in those grim early months at the local school after Gerald Kennard was arrested. They'd shared homework and make-up and illicit outings to pop concerts and talked boys and saving the planet endlessly. But Ally had always been focused on her writing, whereas Hope was only ever focused on foreign travel.

She texted back. *London. Where U?*

Ally, it seemed, was in London too, and knew the perfect wine bar for them to meet and catch up. Hope went.

Ally was sitting at one end of the bar, cradling a half-empty glass with a lot of ice in it and listening raptly to a woman playing jazz piano. She waved when she saw Hope, picked up the bottle of wine and two glasses in front of her, and headed to a table in the corner. They hugged and sat down, grinning like loons.

'It feels like skiving off,' said Hope. 'I keep thinking we ought to keep our hoods up in case Mr Carter sees us.'

Ally poured wine and pushed one glass towards her. 'It's great being a grown-up. And so good to see you. Bit of a surprise, though. I thought you were staying indefinitely in wherever it was.'

'San Michele. No.'

'Exhausted the possibilities? Or were you run out of town?'

'Somewhere between the two.'

Ally cocked her head, just as she always used to at school when she detected a story. She must be a very good journalist, thought Hope suddenly, and wondered why it hadn't occurred to her before.

'Sounds exciting. Want to talk about it?'

'Not really. Tell me about *Celebrity* magazine and your brilliant career.'

Ally pulled a face. 'Not so brilliant at the moment. There's a new editor. We aren't simpatico.'

'That's tough.'

'That's life. You've had your share of working for dweebs, too. What happened in San Michele then? Another employer's friend with wandering hands?'

'No. Forget about it. It's boring. What's wrong with the editor?'

'Oh, he wants me to change the whole thrust of my interviews. Dig up dirt on the people I write about.'

Hope grimaced. She'd been on the receiving end of dirt digging and knew how hurtful it could be. 'Nasty. What are you going to do?'

Ally shrugged. 'Live with him for the moment and carry on doing what I've always done. He may improve once he gets over the urge to plaster his pawprint all over the magazine.'

'And if not?'

'It won't be easy, but there are other jobs. I've got a decent name now.'

'I'll bet you have,' said Hope, pleased and just a little bit envious.

Ally was quick as a whip. 'What is it?'

'Oh nothing. Just someone saying to me today that I have no qualifications and no skills. You've got both, by the bucketful.'

Ally snorted. 'And you've got so many I can't count. And I'm not getting into the mutual self-denigration game. Have some more wine. Who was this rude person?'

'Caroline Grace. We've always called her Aunt Cindy. And she's given me a job for the summer, so less of the 'rude person'. If you please.'

'Caroline Grace the wedding planner?'

'Yes.' Hope was surprised. 'Do you know her?'

'Heard of her,' said Ally thoughtfully. 'She's very well thought of. Classy and discreet rather than the big splash wedding, if you know what I mean.'

'That's good to hear. I was beginning to wonder what I'd got myself into.' And she told Ally the story of the sub-aqua wedding, and they laughed so much they finished the bottle.

Later — over fish and chips in a greasy spoon because Hope had said she hadn't had proper British fish and chips for three years — Ally said, 'Found somewhere to live yet? Or are you staying with Aunt Cindy?'

Hope shook her head. 'She likes her privacy and so do I. I've got a couple of rooms in shared flats to look at tomorrow evening.'

'Well, if that's what you're looking for, I might have an idea. An old colleague of mine has just had an emergency posting to Rome. He doesn't want to leave his flat empty. He rang me up and pretty much begged me to move in and caretake. I really haven't got time to move all my stuff. But you'd be ideal. Want to meet him?'

Hope did.

So Ally made the call and he invited them over at once.

The flat was small and untidy, but then the guy was packing. He was leaving on the Eurostar the next morning. He pretty much fell on Hope's neck with relief at Ally's suggestion, gave her the key, showed her the house folder with all the machine details in it, including the burglar alarm, and invited her to move in as soon as she wanted. Then pretty much shooed them out.

On the pavement, as Hope took note of the street and the bus stops, Ally said, 'He must be really something.'

'What? Who?'

'Mr It's-too-boring-to-talk-about.'

Hope stopped dead as if she'd walked into a wall. She swallowed. 'Why do you say that?'

'Because you didn't even notice Neil, even though he had his shirt half off and is the hottest thing in landlords you'll ever come across.'

'Oh,' said Hope in a small voice. There was no point in denying it. Ally knew her — and human nature — too well.

'So he was hot?'

'Very,' said Hope. She suddenly shivered with longing. It shocked her. Longing was not good. She was supposed to have got over longing.

Ally saw it. Her teasing tone changed. 'It was serious, then?'

Hope nodded. 'Yes.' It was all she had the voice for.

'Ah.' Ally took her by the arm. 'Let's walk. It's cold. Do you need to talk about this?'

Hope swallowed and shook her head.

But back at Ally's and nursing a mug of hot chocolate frothed to bubble-bath proportions, she said, 'I was a real idiot, Ally. I saw this man, he called me a dryad and I — just sort of fell in love, I suppose.' *Though I didn't realize it until it was over.*

'Dryad? Cool.'

Hope's laugh broke in the middle.

Ally sighed in sympathy. 'Did you fall hard?'

'Total immersion.' Hope tried to smile and didn't make a very good job of it.

'So what went wrong?'

'He lied.'

She waited for Ally to pile in with shock, sympathy and censure. But her friend disappointed her.

Instead she said slowly, 'I know how you feel about that, Hope. And I understand. I really do. But it's not so black and white for most of us.'

'What do you mean?'

'There's a spectrum.'

Hope's lip curled. 'Of lies?'

Ally flung up a hand before Hope could say what she thought of that. 'No, I'm not channelling your dad. I'm just saying. There's the white lie where you don't tell your favourite aunt that her cooking is terrible. And then there's the big one, the lie in pursuit of power or profit.'

Hope winced.

Ally nodded soberly. She didn't say 'like your dad's lies'. She didn't need to.

Hope's chin lifted. 'That's different.'

'My point exactly. Be more precise. What did this chap actually lie about? A wife and three children back home in Birmingham?'

'Of course not.' Hope was outraged. 'I'm not a complete fool.'

'So you googled him?'

Hope flushed. 'No.'

'Why not?'

'You know why not.'

'Because bad things were said about you, so you don't trust social media, the press or gossip. Yes, I know.' Ally was kind but she was sticking to her guns. 'So how did you know there wasn't a wife and children?'

'I'm not *that* bad a judge of character.'

'You were never a bad judge of character. Just a tiny bit over-suspicious, maybe. Completely understandable. Which, you have to admit, makes it really interesting that you weren't suspicious of Mr It's-too-boring-to-talk-about.'

Hope gasped. 'I can't believe you just

said that. What happened to sisterly solidarity?'

'Still here. Just got the blinkers off.'

'He *lied* to me.'

'But not about a hidden family he wasn't telling you about.'

Hope gave a snort. 'That's where you're wrong.' She gave Ally a crisp outline of Jonas's deception. But even that didn't seem to convince her friend.

'People suppress stuff for different reasons, Hope. You have to see the whole picture.'

In a goaded voice, Hope said, 'He didn't want me to know he was really a prince.'

Ally nodded. 'Not nice,' she allowed. 'But maybe he wanted a holiday from being a prince and you were his best chance. You need to talk to him about that.'

Hope made a sizzling noise. 'No I don't. I need to forget him and get reacquainted with myself.'

Ally put an arm round her shoulders and squeezed gently. 'I reckon you know yourself pretty well. I'd be surprised if you fell *hard* for someone who didn't tell the truth about important stuff. You've got the best con-man antennae I've ever seen.'

Hope shook her head. 'You know your trouble? You're just a hopeless romantic.'

Ally pretended to be affronted. 'Me? Hardboiled journalist to my fingertips.'

They both laughed, sisterly solidarity restored.

But as Hope was leaving, Ally hugged her and said, 'Last word on the subject, I promise. You want to know what I think? I think you have unfinished business with the Serene Highness.' And she pushed her out of the door before she could argue.

Hope had treated herself to a cab since it was so late, and now she sat in the dark behind the silent driver, thinking. Well, mainly remembering Jonas. His easy familiarity with the forest. His strength. His tenderness that night on the bridge. She hugged her coat around her, remembering the feel of his jacket, still warm from his body. His passion. Their shared laughter. Until that awful night at the ball, she would have said that she had never known anyone as deeply as she knew Jonas. But their intimacy had all been an illusion.

Or had it?

Could Ally have a point?

* * *

By the time Jonas drove the hire car into Combe St Philip, he'd got used to driving on the wrong side of the road again. He hadn't got used to eccentric British signposting, though. It was a relief to find that Hasebury Hall had a decent-sized sign, with *Landscape Gardening* in the bottom right-hand corner and *Corporate Plants* in the left. This was definitely the place.

He drove in past impressive monumental gateposts and up a drive that curved round to the front of the house. He rang the bell. There was no answer.

The house looked deserted.

On impulse, Jonas got back into the car and drove round the house. A shingled path led to a couple of substantial glasshouses. There was definitely movement there.

He parked and got out. A tall man came hurrying towards him, stripping off workmanlike gardener's gloves as he came.

'Hello there. Sorry, I don't hear the bell out here. Max Kennard. Did we have an appointment?'

Jonas braced himself. 'No. We — that is, I know your sister Hope, Sir Max.'

There was a long, nerve-killing silence. Max Kennard didn't offer to shake hands. He didn't offer anything. He just stood there, his cordiality draining away like water out of a leaky bucket, and stared, narrow-eyed. Then he said abruptly, 'You'd better come in.'

He led the way into the house. Jonas noted that it was shabby and could do with a lick of paint, but the panelling in the study gleamed with the patina of years of loving care. Sir Max flung himself into a chair behind the big desk and waved at Jonas to sit down. He didn't offer him a drink.

'So,' he said at last, 'are you the forester?'

Jonas jumped. 'I suppose I am,' he said slowly. 'She's told you about me?'

'Not since she's been home. Hasn't said a word. She mentioned you in a couple of emails before.'

Jonas nodded. 'I see.'

'She liked you. Then.' It sounded like a death knell to Jonas.

He swallowed. 'I know.'

Max swung round and looked out of the window. Clouds were racing across the sky. 'Storm coming,' he said irrelevantly. 'What do you want?'

'I need to see Hope.'

'She isn't here.'

'I *need* to see her,' Jonas said again, suddenly desperate.

'If you think I'm going to tell you where she is, you can forget it.'

Jonas could hardly blame him. 'I hurt

her. I didn't think. It was stupid. I knew how she felt about, well, about lies. She told me about your father. How she loved him but she couldn't trust him and it tore her apart. I knew that. And I thought . . . The stuff I didn't tell her . . . None of it *mattered*, not compared with *us*.' He struck his fist into the palm of his hand. 'How could I have done that?' he said, almost to himself. 'Why didn't I see?'

He looked up. And saw that Max's expression had changed. Oh, he still looked as if he would throw Jonas out of the window at the slightest provocation. But there was something else there, too. A sort of questioning.

As if to confirm it, Max said, 'She told you about our father?'

'Yes.'

'*All* about our father?'

'I don't know,' said Jonas, too exhausted to pretend.

'Did she tell you she visited him in that place?'

Jonas nodded.

'Well that's a first,' said Max unexpectedly.

'What?'

'Normally she just gives 'em the press cuttings and leaves 'em to get on with it. Her men,' he added, in case he hadn't been clear. 'No explanation, no excuse, that's my Hopey.'

Jonas sat bolt upright. *No, she's MY Hope.* His reaction was instant, possessive and probably childish. It didn't make any difference. *She's mine.* God, where had that come from? Was he a caveman now?

Max still looked grumpy, but there was a glimmer of sympathy there too. He said, 'I'm not going to tell you where she is. You'll have to phone her.'

'She's blocked my calls.'

Max sat back. 'Then I can't help you.'

* * *

Jonas drove slowly out between the stone columns. He almost headed straight back to the motorway and London. But then he thought, *I've been driving since the plane landed. I'd better have something to eat.*

He bought a sandwich and wandered round the village. There was an ancient church backing onto the Hasebury Hall estate. He went inside. It had that faint English ecclesiastical smell that he remembered from Cambridge — a mixture of brass polish, freshly laundered surplices, flowers and candlewax. 'Maybe a dash of frankincense,' said Jonas aloud, propping himself up against a pitted stone wall.

There was what looked like a very old stained-glass window. A typed notice underneath read 'Ralph Kennard, merchant'. There was more about the church and the Kennards in a page from a magazine pinned to the church noticeboard. The byline was Ally Parker. *Ally.* The best friend she had gone to school with. The one who was always going to be a writer. The one who had seen her through the bad times.

Maybe she had found sanctuary with Ally Parker.

Well, if Ms Parker was still a journalist, she would be traceable, thought Jonas. And might be persuaded to help. He binned the last of his sandwich and set out for London.

10

By the end of May, Hope felt she was starting to know what she was doing as a wedding planner. She had met dressmakers, caterers, and venue managers and learned how they worked.

She had also met three brides, five mothers-in-law, two overexcited flower girls and one best man. ('Needs watching,' said Natalya. 'Nice chap, complete fruit loop. You'd better take charge of the rings. Get them off him as soon as you can.') She'd hired a stretch limo for a father's partying guests to travel from London to the country church and a horse-drawn open carriage for a Regency bride's two-mile journey from her home.

'You're doing great,' Natalya told her. 'Now go and see if you can find a Harry Potter type venue in or near London that's feasible for a hundred and fifty guests. So no mainline station platforms need apply.'

'Harry Potter?'

'Think Gothic. Basically we're after Leadenhall Market without the smell of cheese.'

'But I don't know London,' said Hope, harassed. 'I've never lived here before. Just stayed over with friends.'

'Just as well. You'll approach it with an open mind. Maybe ask those friends of yours if they have any ideas. Go explore.' And as Hope set off, she called after her, 'No need to come into the office again until Friday. But be here first thing for the Somerset wedding. I suspect we may need to corral that vicar. He had a nasty sermonizing look in his eye and the father-in-law is a militant atheist.'

Hope waved and promised to be back in good time. She was getting a name for being Good with Vicars. It amused her but she felt pleased with herself, too. She thought how it would make Jonas laugh and pushed the thought away at once. It was no good loving the way a man laughed if you couldn't trust him to tell you the truth.

Only what if Ally was right and he had told her all the *important* truths? When she thought about it, he'd only lied by *not* telling her that he was royal. But maybe being a prince was insignificant to him, like being able to ride a bicycle or not liking cheese. Maybe it was only Hope, with her fear of being the centre of attention, who thought being royal was a big deal.

Was it possible?

* * *

Hope was still drawing a blank with the Gothic wedding venue. So she followed Natalya's advice and texted the problem to her friends.

They arranged to meet for breakfast, because that was the only time Flora Deare could manage. She was staying overnight with Ally after a mysterious meeting that both Hope and Ally suspected was with her ex-boyfriend. Flora wasn't telling. All she would say was that she had to get home to Combe St Philip to relieve her elderly grandfather's carer.

So they took a picnic into Green Park. That was Hope's idea. She was missing trees. Well, that was what she told her friends. Though she'd lived in lots of cities and never missed trees before.

The truth was, she was missing Jonas. She wouldn't have admitted it to anyone else, but she faced the truth herself. Ever since Ally had said the dread words 'unfinished business', she hadn't been able to get him out of her mind.

She even unblocked his number on her phone. But he didn't call. She had a sleepless night, constantly waking, wondering what time it was in San Michele and then falling back into a half-doze. Sometime before dawn she fell into an exhausted sleep, only to jerk awake reaching for her phone before her eyes were properly open. And then she realized that it was the alarm clock.

'This is ridiculous,' she shouted.

And blocked Jonas's number again. She needed her sleep. The job was demanding. Besides, that was the morning she, Ally and Flora were having their breakfast picnic in the park.

They met early. The June light was golden but not yet warm, and there was still dew on the grass. So they colonized one of the park benches. Flora handed out wonderful crisp and flaky palmiers she had made herself and Ally opened a bottle of Buck's Fizz. Hope had brought coffee from home.

'Not in the same class,' she said ruefully, accepting pastry and fizz.

'Who cares? It's wet and warm,' said Ally. It sounded as if she were making an effort to be cheerful.

She was looking strained, with great shadows under her eyes. But she said nothing and Hope didn't want to grill her. Instead she said, 'I'm getting to feel that this Gothic wedding venue is my Waterloo. Any ideas?'

Flora knew a little about catered

events and had worked in a London restaurant. She mused aloud on a couple of names but one was too large and the other was, well, 'A bit S&M, to be honest,' said Flora. 'More vampires and zombies than weddings, if you know what I mean. Unless they *want* a zombie wedding?'

'I can't honestly see my Aunt Cindy running a zombie wedding. She's more three-row string of pearls and a big hat, if you know what I mean.'

Even Ally cheered up at that. When they stopped laughing she said, 'There might be some places outside London.'

But Hope didn't think that would run, so they stopped worrying about it and just gossiped. By that time the sun was a lot warmer.

'Let's move to the grass,' said Flora, packing up neatly. 'I'll have to go soon, but I'd like to take my shoes off and get my feet in the grass just once before I go.'

'I'll get more coffee,' said Ally, jumping to her feet. 'They'll be open in

Piccadilly now. What do you want, Flora? I know Hope's an Americano, single shot.'

Flora opted for the same and Ally strode off, dodging joggers as they laboured up the slight hill behind the eighteenth-century mansions to reach Green Park Underground station.

'Can you imagine doing that?' asked Flora, peacefully surveying the runners as she wiggled her bare toes in the grass. 'Fancy going into work all hot and sweaty. And on a beautiful day like this. Horrible.'

'I suppose they enjoy it.' Hope studied the passers-by. 'I mean that guy looks quite an athlete.'

He was powering along away from the underground against the flow, on the outside of the path. He moved beautifully, rhythmically, as if all his joints were oiled and fresh and his feet were on springs.

Flora studied him dispassionately. 'He's hot,' she allowed.

But Hope was coming slowly to her

feet. *As if all his joints were oiled*. It was Jonas. It had to be him. *I know those thighs*, she thought distractedly. And she knew that look, too: the focused, straight-ahead, I-can-get-this-done look.

Jonas was *here*! Not in San Michele, with his brother the crown prince and his sister-in-law, the gracious crown princess, who'd looked as if she'd been born wearing a tiara. He was here in London.

Looking for her?

No. Not looking for her. He had no idea she was in England, let alone London. So he must be in London for some other purpose. And he was in the park to exercise, like all the other early-morning athletes. He was staring straight ahead. He wouldn't even see her unless she accosted him.

Her heart turned into a ball of ice and started bouncing in time with his pounding feet. Was she going to accost him? She could just keep her head down, carry on talking to Flora and Ally when she returned, and pretend that she hadn't seen him. No one need ever know.

But — unfinished business? Whatever else she might be, she wasn't a coward. This was her chance to find out if Ally might be right, after all. Or just to talk to him. Maybe he was hurting as much as she was. She couldn't bear that.

Hope began to move towards the runners' path as if she were hypnotized. Flora sat up. 'Hope . . . ?'

But Hope was already raising an arm, waving, calling out, 'Jonas. *Jonas.*'

The runner missed his stride, staggered forward and came to a stop. He looked round wildly.

She ran towards him. Jonas found her. He vaulted over the guard rail and sprinted across the grass to meet her. They both stopped at the same time, two feet apart. For a crazy moment she was overwhelmed with gladness.

Jonas found his voice first. 'Hope. How are you here?' He sounded stunned.

She didn't know what to say, so she answered the question literally. 'Having a picnic with my friends. You?'

Jonas seemed to pull himself together. He pushed his hand through his hair in a gesture that was so familiar. Something twisted under her breastbone.

'I'm in London on a case. And spending all my free time trying to work out how to get you to see me. Or at least start taking my calls,' he said with a rueful smile.

Oh that smile! But he didn't sound as if he were lying this time. And here came the memory of that last horrible scene in the statue garden, crowding in at last, too late.

He must have sensed her withdrawal, because he put out a hand. 'Do I look too disreputable to meet your friends?'

She should have said yes. She should have wished him a pleasant run and turned and gone back to Flora.

She said, 'No. They're my two very best friends. I've known them forever. I'd like you to meet them.' And she turned and led him back to Flora on the grass.

By the time Ally came back with the coffees, he and Flora were getting on as if they'd known each other for years. Mind you, Flora had always been a sweetheart, ready to see the best in everybody. And she didn't know about the mystery prince in Hope's life, unless Ally had told her.

Jonas leaped up from the grass as soon as Ally came to a halt beside them and held out his hand to take the coffees from her. 'Hi,' he said. 'Jonas Reval. I don't suppose Hope has mentioned me?'

'No.' Ally's eyes were shrewd. She raised an eyebrow at Hope, who found she was blushing furiously. 'An acquaintance from your travels?'

'Something like that,' Jonas said easily. 'And you must be Ally Parker.'

Hope's head reared up. It sounded as if he already knew the name. Suddenly her old suspicious self was awake and muttering warnings in her ear.

'You know about Ally?' she asked, her eyes narrowed and hostile.

Jonas looked surprised. 'Of course.

You talked about her. Primary school together, right? And then your champion at the comprehensive. And when I was in Combe St Philip I saw an article by her in the church. In fact I've been trying to find a mutual friend to introduce me. It occurred to me you might be staying with her.'

Ally's eyebrows hit her hairline. 'What were you doing in Combe St Philip?'

'Fact-finding,' said Jonas promptly. 'Tourism, that sort of thing.'

His eyes invited Hope to share his amusement. But she was concentrating on something entirely different.

'Me? Staying with her? You've been looking for me?'

'Of course. You blocked my calls. What else could I do? I didn't think you'd like it if I hired a private eye.'

'Good call,' said Ally. She extracted the coffee cups from the cardboard holder that Jonas was still carrying and handed them round.

Hope received hers without thanks

and watched her friends. Jonas was putting himself out to be charming and Flora was responding with all her usual warmth. Something in Hope's heart twisted and she looked away. She wanted to shout, '*No!*'

It hurt like a burn. Flora was so trusting, so open-hearted. Hope wanted to get between them. She swallowed a huge lump in her throat and shut her eyes. When she opened them, she found Ally looking at her, who had clearly put two and two together. She pursed her lips and subjected Jonas to silent scrutiny.

Flora was explaining Hope's difficulties with the Gothic wedding venue and what she and Ally had already suggested.

Jonas looked interested, just as he always did. Sexy and interested. How had she forgotten that intense concentration of his? Was it a deliberate trick? Or genuine? It was certainly flattering. Though level-headed Flora showed no signs of succumbing to, or even noticing, the flattery. And Ally was still considering him dispassionately, as if he were on trial.

So is it only me who melts into a puddle of warm lust when he looks like that? Hope winced.

'Sounds like you need one of those historical walking tours,' he said. 'Someone who will walk you round with an old map and show you the buildings that still survive. I used to take one of those at least once a month when I first came to London. I'll have a dig around and see whether I've still got any of the maps they gave me.'

'Oh that's a great idea,' said Flora, as sunny as always.

Ally was more measured. 'I've heard of those. Certainly worth giving it a go. What do you think, Hope?'

Hope came to herself with a start. Everyone was looking at her. 'I'll think about it,' she said at random.

'Great. I'll sort something out,' said Jonas easily. 'Sunday suit you?'

Hope was glad she could say

truthfully, 'All my weekends are busy. Sorry.' Though even to her own ears she didn't sound sorry.

Sweet Flora looked shocked. 'She really is,' she hastened to assure Jonas. 'This is the height of the wedding season, and they nearly always happen at the weekend.'

He turned that intense, interested look on Hope again. 'Is that what you're doing? Organizing weddings?'

'Working for someone who does.' She smiled with an effort.

'Fine. A weekday then. I'll free up some time in my diary. Can I give you a call this morning? You can tell me when suits you.'

There was no way out. 'Thank you,' she said as graciously as she could manage.

Hope had never felt so conflicted in her life. It had been such a delight to catch sight of him. Her whole being had been swamped with relief and pleasure. She'd thought, *We've got a second chance! Oh thank God, we can try again!*

And then the moment she was close to him, watching him and remembering, she felt all knotted up with mistrust and sadness and, yes, longing, until she couldn't see straight.

Jonas murmured, 'Of course, you'll have to unblock my calls if you want me to help.'

His laughing eyes challenged her to tell him to mind his own business and leave her alone. Hope had no idea why she didn't do just that. Except that it was all too painful and she might give herself away.

He thought it was funny. She could tell from his voice. God help her, he thought she would think it was funny too. She needed to get away before the threatening tears overwhelmed her.

She pressed her lips together and stood up. 'Excuse me. I need to walk.' She didn't wait for a reply. She couldn't afford to. She headed off towards Piccadilly and the Underground, where she could lose herself in the crowd of office workers and early-rising tourists.

She didn't look back.

Behind her, she heard Ally say firmly, 'Cramp. She's a martyr to it.'

Flora chimed in, 'Best leave her to her walk it out, Jonas. She prefers to sort herself out on her own. Always has.'

Thank God for friends.

Even so, she left the park running.

* * *

YES! She'd agreed to unblock his number. Result!

So why didn't he feel better about it?

Her friends were watching him closely. He said, 'I didn't know that.'

Flora said comfortably, 'Have you known her long?'

'Not months and years. But we spent the best part of every day together in the forest for a couple of weeks.'

He didn't say that it had brought them close. The women must have gathered as much from the hungry way he'd been staring at her. Yet after that crazy, wonderful chance meeting, Hope had hardly looked at him. Barely said a word to him. She hadn't laughed once, and he loved her laugh. And she looked as tense as a spring about to snap.

'The forest sounds nice,' said Flora. 'I always think of Hope as a country girl.'

Ally said, 'Hope can do anything she puts her mind to.'

Jonas's head came up and his eyes narrowed. It sounded like a warning. Why should Ms Parker be warning him? Had Hope confided in her? What had she said? Did he really want to know?

Flora looked at her watch. 'Oh heavens. I need to scoot or I'll miss my train. Where are my shoes?'

They found her shoes and Ally said, 'You go. I'll clear up and dump the litter. Lovely to see you. Come back soon.'

They kissed, and Flora sent Jonas a smile of unshadowed friendliness before she scampered off. So it was only Ally who was sending out warnings, he thought. Interesting.

'Let me help.' He gathered up the remnants of the picnic packaging, sorted it into cardboard and plastic piles, and flattened both and put them into a paper bag. 'I'll take it back to the office. We recycle.'

Ally nodded. She had packed all the food and drink remains into a cool bag. He picked it up and prepared to escort her out of the park. 'Thank you,' she said.

'My pleasure.'

They walked up the hill towards Piccadilly. Ally was frowning but polite enough, enquiring where he worked, how long he was going to be in London.

'Ten minutes the other side of Piccadilly. On the lap of the gods. I'm here on a sort of secondment, I suppose you'd say.'

She looked at him quickly. 'So not because of Hope?'

'As far as work is concerned, I stay as

long as the job lasts,' he said carefully.

She digested that. Then she said, 'Be straight with me, if you please. How important is Hope in your future plans?'

He was so astonished that for a moment he couldn't answer.

She gave a faint smile. 'She told me a bit about what's brought her home. I'm assuming it was you.' And added deliberately, 'Your Serene Highness.'

Jonas almost put up a hand to protect himself from a body blow. 'Yes, that's me.' It felt like pleading guilty in a court of law.

But Ally didn't reproach or lecture. She just nodded and stomped on in silence for a little.

When they came in sight of the gate, she stopped and said with resolution, 'Has Hope said anything to you about her family?'

'Her father? Yes.'

'Well, that's good.' She thought for a bit. 'Look, it's none of my business. But I've known her since before her father became a crook.'

He waited. She was clearly torn.

In the end she said, 'Hope doesn't trust anyone. Not after her father. It isn't that she's paranoid or anything. She just — keeps her options open. Especially with strangers.'

Jonas stared. 'But — she trusted me,' he said blankly.

Ally just looked at him. 'Quite.'

And then he saw exactly what he'd done. Why they had sometimes felt so close and yet Hope could throw him back into the middle distance for no reason that he could understand. Why, that night on the bridge, when she put her head on his shoulder and they went back to what felt like home, had been a turning point for her. And he'd spoilt it.

She'd told him about her father's humiliation and her own; her adolescent sense of shame and disappointment in the father she loved; her travels to discover what she was capable of. That had taken courage to do and possibly even more courage for her to share. With him.

And what had he shared with her? Nothing. Well, his love of nature, the forest, the birds. A little about his student life. But his family, his professional life, the stresses of family and national politics? Not a word.

Hope had trusted him. And he'd failed her. Worse than that, he'd betrayed her trust. And she found out in the most horrible way possible. It had all been public.

'Oh my God.'

Ally just nodded and took the cool bag from his resistless fingers. She gave him a friendly buffet to the upper arm. 'Good luck.'

She walked off to work, leaving him staring at the trees, appalled at how much damage he had already done. Would he ever be able to put it right?

11

Hope was sitting with three weary bridesmaids discussing the colour of ribbons when Jonas called. She almost sent it to voicemail. But then she thought, no, better to take this first call in a public place with people she knew on the horizon. That way she could keep it together. So she made apologetic gestures and took herself off to the corner of the dressmaker's workroom.

'Hello, Jonas.' It came out friendly enough but professionally brisk. 'I'm with a client.'

'Tomorrow, eleven o'clock,' he said. 'Meet me at the Monument. I've found the route and my notes. If we do the whole walk, it's two to three hours. Can you manage that?'

She consulted her calendar. 'Eleven's fine. I have a meeting in West London at four, so I may have to leave before 'your tour is over.'

'Your call.'

'Thank you. I'll see you then.'

'Looking forward to it.' He rang off.

Such a short exchange to make her shake convulsively.

The chief bridesmaid saw it. 'Bad news?' she asked in concern.

Hope shook her head. Her teeth were actually chattering. 'A challenging meeting tomorrow.'

They were so sympathetic, they forgot their squabbles over the shade of their ribbons. 'Oh let's just make a decision and go and have some tea,' said the youngest bridesmaid impatiently. 'Toss a coin?'

But Hope persuaded them to write down their first and second choices on two pieces of paper and one absolute veto on another. Then she set them out on a table. One colour had two second favourites and no veto.

'Done,' they all said, with great sighs of relief, and Hope finalized the order with the dressmaker.

'Your decisions seem so easy to make,' said the chief bridesmaid. 'I bet you're super organized.'

'I wish,' said Hope, who hadn't the faintest idea what she was going to say to Jonas on the following day.

She tried writing options down on Post-it notes, to study what her reaction was to them. All that achieved was that she got thoroughly hot and bothered and couldn't eat anything for supper.

The real issue, of course, was whether she demanded at least an explanation, and preferably an apology, for his deception in San Michele. Part of her thought there was no point in holding a post-mortem on a dead love, especially an unacknowledged one. Part of her thought she had a right to know. None of her wanted to broach the subject. And all of her didn't want to risk opening that particular wound again.

She still hadn't decided when she caught the Underground to meet him. She was early at the meeting place, but

Jonas was earlier. She recognized him with a little shock. She had seen him in ranger work clothes, a jacket and jeans when he took her out to dinner, and the chillingly elaborate military uniform at that terrible ball. And, of course, she had seen him naked. But she had never seen or imagined him in an immaculate city suit, with a perfectly cut waistcoat and a jacket lined with olive silk. He looked very handsome, of course, but also alien and rather intimidating.

Well, she wasn't going to let his city suit intimidate her, whatever other stupidity she might find herself committing.

'I didn't realize you were a dandy,' she said as a greeting. The remark also neatly solved the problem of whether to shake hands, kiss or shuffle awkwardly round each other.

Jonas pulled a face. 'My current major client thinks a prince should look like a prince,' he said with great deliberation, watching her carefully.

So the issue was going to be out in

the open, Hope thought. After last night's decision failure and her seriously troubled dreams, it was almost a relief to have the decision taken out of her hands. But she didn't know what to say.

When she didn't answer, he said, 'I'm sorry, Hope.'

She stared and saw, to her surprise, how difficult he was finding this.

'I mean, I'm really, really sorry. About not telling you the full story of who I am. About everything I said and did at that damned ball. I thought I had more time — ' He bit it off. 'But that's no excuse. There *is* no excuse. I just got everything wrong.'

Hope became aware of a real, physical pain in her chest, impeding her breathing. Any moment now the tension was going to close off her lungs completely, and then she'd be gasping and then she'd be weeping and then . . . She couldn't bear it. She flung up a hand.

'Not now.' Her voice was so harsh,

she hardly recognized it.

But Jonas just nodded, as if that was what he'd been expecting. 'If that's what you want, of course.' He brought out his phone and brought up a document. 'Then let's get on with the tour.'

'Thank you,' Hope said in a small voice.

'Starting with The Monument itself. Built to commemorate the Great Fire of London in 1666. It's as tall as the fire stretched. Probably designed by Robert Hooke, though Christopher Wren signed off on the drawings. The fire lasted from Sunday to Wednesday and wiped out everything between here and Pudding Lane.'

They both looked up. It was a simple enough column, but to Hope it seemed immensely high. 'It's bigger than it looks in photographs. I've never seen it in real life before.'

'My grandmother brought me here when I was about seven. She loved London and history, both.'

'You grandmother?'

'My grandmother is English,' he said levelly. 'After my mother died, she brought us up. Probably before, too, come to think of it.'

'How old were you?'

'When my mother died? Four. But she'd been ill for a long time. I don't remember much about her. I've seen her on film, of course.'

'I'm sorry. I didn't know.' But something was niggling at the back of her brain. Surely she *had* known? Or suspected, at least.

But Jonas was waving it away, giving her a smile that didn't reach his eyes. 'Of course you didn't. I didn't tell you. No need to be sorry. My fault entirely. Shall we walk?'

It was like that for the rest of the walk. He was informed, helpful and endlessly patient. He took her to see small enclosed courts with Georgian fountains; narrow cobbled alleys where bow-windowed shops faced each other and old gas lamps presided over the footway; run-down Victorian railway arches and refurbished eighteenth-century factories; even a disused church. Hope took photographs and made notes. Jonas waited without complaining as she did so.

Eventually she closed her phone with an air of finality. 'Right. I've taken in as much as I can for now. It's given me lots to think about. Thank you. That was a revelation.'

This time the smile did light his eyes. It felt good. Even better, Hope found she was smiling back.

'You don't realize how much everyday history is left until you go looking,' he agreed. She looked at her watch. 'May I give you lunch to say thank you?'

He hesitated. 'I thought you had a meeting?'

'Client cancelled.'

'Really?'

'Really.' She paused. 'Well, with a tiny amount of encouragement from me, to be honest. When it became clear that the bridegroom couldn't make it.'

Jonas raised an eyebrow.

'His mother had volunteered to represent him. The bride sounded frantic.' Her tone was carefully neutral.

He laughed, then. 'Sounds like a major diplomatic dispute.'

'It was for the bride. Not me. I just said it was company policy and offered to go over to see them any evening when the bridegroom is home. He's going to text me.'

'I'm impressed. So — lunch, then.'

Jonas sent a quick text and then took her back to a small Italian place they had already passed on the walk. Whether by accident or design, they were shown to a discreet alcove table. Hope suspected design.

The waiter brought menus but Hope had already started looking at her notes, flicking through the photos she had taken on her phone.

'Shall I order for us both? You're too wired to concentrate. What sort of thing would you like?'

'Anything. Just lots.' She looked up and grinned then.

For a moment his face, his whole body, went absolutely still.

Hope raised an eyebrow. 'Why are you looking like that? I'm starving.'

'Glad to hear it. And this is my shout, by the way. I enjoyed our walk. It got me out of the office when I really needed it.'

She went back to her notes, frowning and muttering. Jonas took her at her word, ordering olives and wine first, then a pasta dish to be followed by cutlets and every vegetable on the menu. She absently helped herself to an olive when it arrived and carried on zipping between shots on her phone.

'You know what I think might work? If we took over a whole Victorian alley. We'd need to persuade the shopkeepers to co-operate, of course. It wouldn't work anywhere that Saturday is the major shopping day of the week. Nowhere central. But somewhere a bit off the beaten track . . . ' She finished the olives. She hadn't touched the wine. 'What do you think?'

'It's your area of expertise, not mine.'

'Well, what would you think if you were a guest?'

'I'd think it was original and fun,' he said honestly.

She nodded. 'Me too. I might really have something here.'

'Let's drink to it,' he said, taking her hand and curving it round the stem of her wine glass. 'It's better than San Michele supermarket red.'

For a moment she didn't understand him. Then she remembered their night in the hut, the rough wine in the mugs, the firelight . . . She flushed to the roots of her hair and dropped her phone.

Jonas raised his glass to her, locking eyes. 'Congratulations on a working hypothesis.'

'Er — thank you,' she said, breaking the eye contact to retrieve the phone.

The waiter brought their *pasta alla Norma*.

'So how have you got into the

wedding business?'

She told him, between squeaks of appreciation at the perfectly crisped aubergine.

'Do you enjoy it?'

'Not to begin with,' she said honestly. 'I was out of my depth, and anyway, I was way out of love with coupledom.'

'Yes, I can see that you might be.' His voice was dark with regret.

She wasn't up to dealing with that yet. She said bracingly, 'But then I got to see that it was just like organizing anything else. You don't have to buy into the hearts and flowers side. You just need a budget and a deadline and an agreed brief.'

There was a pause. Jonas seemed troubled. Hope looked at him levelly.

At last he said, 'That doesn't sound very romantic.' He was half-amused, half-reproachful.

Her eyes skidded away from him. She shrugged.

'What's the most difficult thing about it?'

'Getting people to make up their mind. And then sticking to it, I suppose. But just getting them to shut the door on all the other options can be a nightmare.'

'Is that what you thought I was doing when I didn't tell you what I was?' It seemed to burst out of him. 'Not making up my mind?'

Hope looked away. 'Maybe.'

Jonas shook his head. 'No. It wasn't like that. You have to believe me, Hope. It was never that.'

'No foul if it was. Neither of us was talking commitment, were we? Hell, we were hardly talking at all.' Hope heard the brittle words with dismay. She sounded so hard, so careless. She almost called them back. But then she thought of where that might take her, and clamped her lips shut. She wasn't ready for this yet. If she ever would be.

Jonas shook his head. 'It felt as if we were talking all the time,' he said quietly. 'Words, no words, it was all the same. To me, anyway. I've never felt so

— right — with anyone.' He hesitated. Then squared his shoulders and said, 'I thought you felt it too.'

And that floored her. She just stared at him, her eyes filling, her heart pounding in her ears, an inner voice screaming, *No, No, NO!*

She stuffed her phone into her bag and jumped to her feet. 'I need to go. Thank you for showing me the cobbled places. Very helpful. Thank you for lunch, too. I'll — Goodbye.'

And she fled.

★　★　★

Jonas walked back to the office. It took him an hour. It would have been better to take a cab. But he needed to sort his head out.

When Hope had called to him in the park, it had not only been a shock, he had felt an instant wave of thankfulness too, so strong that it had almost felt like being drunk. His first thought was, *She's forgiven me!* Of course, he'd realized almost at once that it was more complicated than that. But at least she was talking to him, even friendly, in a careful, slightly distant way. And she introduced him to her best friends. He was being given a second chance. He didn't deserve it, but he was so thankful he could have kissed everybody in Green Park for joy.

But then Hope had slipped away, and Ally Parker had laid the situation on the line for him. For the first time, he saw what he'd done in San Michele in pitiless perspective.

He'd failed Hope. Failed her badly. And then today, he had seen, really *seen* beyond any possibility of doubt just how much he'd hurt her. And, worse, what it had done to her. He was horrified at himself. How could he have been so blind?

Hope had changed in just a few weeks. She'd gone from a free-spirited dryad in shirt and jeans to a well-groomed businesswoman with guarded eyes.

Oh, it wasn't just the smart clothes and the sophisticated manner. Even with her friends yesterday, Hope had seemed quieter, less spontaneous than he remembered. But today he'd seen real wariness in her eyes, not just towards him, but when she talked about her work. The brave, laughing woman he'd known in San Michele forest had gone into deep cover.

And it was his fault.

So it was his responsibility to rescue the dryad in Hope Kennard. Before it was too late.

12

Jonas took time to think about the next step. It was too important to rush into, he told himself. He had to be sure he was doing the right thing, especially for Hope. Though it was hard to curb his instinct to call her, especially in the early morning when she wasn't there, her red-gold hair a tumble on his pillow.

He woke up in his discreetly luxurious hotel room every day feeling that something was wrong. Then he remembered. And the ache started. And the restlessness.

He prowled the room. He went running. He worked like a demon, even replying to the Very Difficult Client's midnight texts by return.

'You know, we could do with you here in London permanently,' said the senior partner of their London Associates. 'Or at least as long as Danilov stays on this seek-and-destroy mission. You're the only one he listens to. How would you feel about a longer secondment?'

It would buy him more time close to Hope. 'I'll talk to my brothers. See if we can work something out.'

Carlo, when Jonas approached him, was disappointed but philosophical. 'I'm not really surprised. And it would be good to stay tight with Penrys. Are you're sure you don't mind, though?'

'It suits me very well at the moment,' Jonas said honestly.

'Then let's do it.' Carlo added in a gruff voice, 'We'll miss you. Especially the kids.'

'Me too,' said Jonas, touched. Carlo had never said they'd miss him before.

And then, at last, Jonas called Hope.

'I need advice.'

She was friendly enough but distant. 'What sort of advice?'

'My secondment's been extended. I don't want to stay in a hotel ad infinitum. I need to look for a place to rent.'

She disclaimed all experience. 'You want Ally. She found me my flat.'

The best laid plans, thought Jonas, laughing at himself in the mirror. But he recovered fast. 'Well I really need a second pair of eyes. Someone to double-check my decision.'

'Why?' She sounded curious rather than suspicious.

'I don't think I'm very good at recognizing my own instincts,' he said ruefully.

'Ah.'

'And you know me better than anyone else in London. What I like, what's important to me. Things I might forget or overlook. Ally doesn't.'

She considered in silence. Jonas waited hopefully.

'All right,' she said at last. 'I'll be your quality control backup. But no weekends, remember.'

Jonas agreed a date with her and organized an estate agent to show them half a dozen apartments.

The June weather had gone from

distinctly wet and chilly to blazing hot. Hope came to meet him in the park near Penrys's building. The grass was full of people stripping down to a decent minimum and splashing bottled water over their pink skin.

'The trouble is, it doesn't last,' said Hope, watching them with sympathy. 'It dries instantly and then you feel hotter than ever.'

'London is not the best place to experience warm weather,' he agreed.

She snorted. For a moment she sounded like Dryad Hope again. 'Experience *warm* weather indeed! This is hot, you pampered foreigner. Hot, hot, HOT.'

'You only think that because it's so humid.'

'I think that because it was too hot to sleep last night and I've been ratty all day as a result.'

'Your apartment has no air conditioning?'

'My apartment is a conversion. Third floor of an Edwardian villa. Its windows open. That's the air conditioning.'

'But that is terrible, in this weather. You boil or you're deafened by the traffic.'

She narrowed her eyes at him. 'But very, very green. You ought to approve of that, Conservation Guy.'

He groaned and she laughed aloud, doing a little dance of triumph round him on the courtyard.

'I win. I win.'

He was so pleased to see her laughing and dancing again that he didn't even try to defend himself. 'You do indeed.'

They met the agent at the first apartment, a cool Scandinavian-influenced open plan in a newly built block. It had air conditioning.

'It's also silent as the grave. Does anybody actually live here?' asked Hope, clearly in fighting form.

The agent muttered about investment property and river views.

Hope rounded on Jonas. 'Do you think it feels like a home?'

He had to admit it didn't. 'But then I

don't have much concept of home. I've always lived above the shop, as it were.'

Hope frowned. 'Huh?'

'It always had to be clean and tidy because it was a work space. You never knew who might arrive to — er — do business. Definitely no feet on the furniture.'

She went rather quiet after that.

They looked at two more, one a great deal more luxurious with a heated pool in the basement, but otherwise very similar to the unhomely first candidate.

Hope started to look mulish. 'Don't you have any with trees? A hedge? Anything with its roots in the soil?'

The agent looked uneasily at Jonas. 'There's one with a rooftop terrace. It's got trees now, as it happens. But they're in tubs, and the outgoing tenant was complaining about the cost of mainte-nance. It's included in the rental price.'

'We'll look,' Jonas decided.

Hope loved it. It was the penthouse, and the roof terrace ran the whole width of the block. It had planters with scented-leaved shrubs, four substantial birch trees in wide containers, and a picnic area furnished with enough garden furniture to seat a Boy Scout troop. There was also a fountain. The agent found the switch and turned it on. When it was dark, there would be lights in the trees as well, but it was really the fountain that sold it to Hope, Jonas saw.

'It's wonderful,' she breathed. 'And if you can't sleep indoors, you can just come outside and sleep on that sofa.'

'Mmm.' Jonas curbed his imagination. Hope wasn't issuing an invitation, and anyway, they were not alone. *Got to do something about that low flashpoint*, he thought. 'I'll take it,' he said, giving the agent his business card. 'Email me the papers tomorrow and I'll sign and transfer whatever funds you need. I'd like to move in at the weekend.'

They all left together. Once they'd said goodbye to the agent outside the building, Hope turned distant again.

She refused his invitation to dinner.

'Another time,' she said just a little too briskly to be wholly believable. 'We've got a complicated wedding this week, and I've got some essential handicrafts to do tonight. *And* an ultra-early start tomorrow morning as well.'

Jonas's brain was working at warp speed. He was recalling that joyful confidence in herself that Hope had brought to San Michele and he, heaven help him, seemed to have undermined. He remembered how proud she had been of her independence, of the skills she had mastered on her travels. And now she was working all hours on other people's weddings, while stubbornly determined to stay unromantic and talking about budgets instead of love. It was a wicked waste.

What could he do, though? He had no right to criticize her. But those long hours, though. Maybe he could do something there. Help her out with her wedding tasks, the way she had helped

him on his ranger duties. That was how
they had got close in the first place,
after all. His blood began to quicken.

He said in a casual voice, 'Anything I
can do? Very willing to lend a hand.'

'You? But you've got a full-time job!'

'My hours are flexible,' he assured
her. 'And I've already proved my worth
with your search for a Gothic London
venue, haven't I?'

She was not convinced. 'Possibly.'

'Oh come on. You had at least two
good candidates there.'

She laughed. 'Fair enough. But I
don't see you sewing bridesmaids'
headdresses, which is what I'm doing
tonight.'

Jonas quailed. But he really needed
to get her to commit to the next
meeting. So whatever it took. 'I can try,'
he said heroically.

She shook her head. 'Much quicker if
I do it myself. 'But — ' She surveyed
him with speculation. 'Do you have a
car?'

'Yes.' It wasn't quite a lie, he told

himself. So far he hadn't bothered to rent a car in central London, but if Hope could use him with a car, then a car he would hire and hold at her disposal as soon as possible.

'Well, I've got to go to the market to buy flowers for the wedding. The trouble is, I need to get there terribly early. Aunt Cindy said half past four.'

So that meant hiring a car tonight. He'd go off to the rental office the moment she said goodbye.

'I can do that. Where is it? And more important, where do I pick you up?'

'New Covent Garden. You'll find a map online.'

'OK. Your address?'

She told him.

'I know that area. It's not too far from where I lived when I first came to London. What about I pick you up at four? There'll be minimal traffic at that time of day. We'll get there in fifteen minutes from you, tops.'

'*Thank* you.' She beamed.

Jonas felt it through to his bones.

God, he loved her when she was like this, brimming with enthusiasm and eagerness for the task in hand. He wanted to hug her so much it hurt.

He kept his hands by his sides and a casual smile pinned to his face like concrete. 'Great. You have my number. Call me if there are any problems.'

'You too,' she said. 'You may just have saved my life. See you tomorrow.'

And she shot into the crowd and away.

Jonas let out a long, wondering breath. Maybe, just maybe, there was light at the end of the tunnel.

* * *

Hope had changed out of her pretty summer dress, which Jonas hadn't noticed at all, she was certain, and was in shorts and a strappy top when the doorbell rang.

She half thought it might be Jonas and picked up the entry phone with mingled trepidation and — dammit

— longing, again. But it turned out to be Ally, bearing snacks and wine and in need of a chat. Hope, facing several hours of making bridesmaids' garlands, welcomed her with open arms.

Ally sank down on the carpet beside Hope and picked over twisty gold wire and felt rosebuds. 'Good grief. We are doing this? Why?'

'The mother-in-law ordered them. She forgot to say they were for grown-up bridesmaids.' Hope held up a kindergarten-sized coronet. 'The mother of the bride is not amused. She intends to Have Words.'

Ally gave a squawk of laughter. 'The marriage totters?'

'Well, it's certainly going to need aftercare, if I can't sort this out.'

'Can't you just lose the things? They're pretty naff.'

'Mother-in-law bought them,' Hope repeated patiently. She sighed. 'Of course, in principle you're right. That's exactly what the bride said. Before she kicked the wastepaper basket to pulp

310

and burst into tears, that is.'

'You can't blame her.'

'I don't. Which is why I'm trying to make replacements.'

Ally looked at her with fascination. 'Do you *know* how to make replacements?'

'I do now,' said Hope grimly. 'Three YouTube tutorials, half a dozen DIY wedding blogs and Natalya's written instructions.'

The first one was a bit ragged. They got better. Ally piled into a multi-layered salad and salami and Hope opened the wine. The garlands started to look a lot more relaxed after that.

In the middle of all the stabbing and twisting, Ally said, 'So that was Mr Too-boring-to-talk-about. I like him.'

Hope stiffened. 'It showed. Of course, he can be very charming.'

'Ah. And the charm might work on me, innocent that I am. But now you're armoured against it?'

Hope laughed, blushed, reached for her wine glass and looked sheepish.

'You've got me. Not armoured at all.'

Ally's eyes sharpened. 'So you won't be seeing him anymore?'

'Not *exactly*.'

'Your armour's evaporated and you're back in each other's arms?'

Hope was affronted. 'Certainly not. I'm not that much of a fool. I'm just being civil.'

'How civil?'

Hope gave a choke of laughter. 'Actually he's the one being civil, when I come to think about it. I've lined him up to help me collect rosebuds and other assorted flowers from New Covent Garden tomorrow. He's picking me up. At 4.00 a.m.'

Ally gulped. 'That's *seriously* civil,' she agreed faintly.

'So between you, it looks as if I might actually get a couple of hours' sleep tonight after all.'

'Glad to oblige, ma'am.'

They finished the garlands and applied themselves to the chocolate. And then it was so late that Ally stayed the night on Neil's sofa. Hope left her there, when she tiptoed out to collect the waiting rosebuds.

Jonas was waiting in the street beside a gleaming Mercedes. He got out as soon as he saw her come out of the front door and opened the passenger door for her. He didn't offer to kiss her, but she thought it was a near-run thing, and her heart warmed.

'You're early,' they both said in unison.

'I wasn't going to ring the doorbell until the allotted time,' Jonas said. 'I used to live in a place like that. Entry phone or no, everyone in the house always hears it.'

Hope smiled at him with approval. 'That's what I thought. I was going to sit on the steps and wait for you.'

'Couple of good citizens, we are.' He closed the door on her and got in.

'This is a crazy car to drive in London, but I'm really glad you do. I need a car with a nice big boot. My shopping list is longer than I'd realized. The flowers are going to take up a lot of space.'

Jonas seemed to take a decision. 'I'm

not telling any more lies, not even white ones, not even about trivia. I hired this car last night. It was all they had.'

Hope burst out laughing, although she had felt a bit uncomfortable at the reference to lies. 'Then it's my lucky day.'

She was right. It took the best part of a couple of hours to buy everything on the list. By the time they'd loaded everything, they'd filled the boot and the back seat too with long brown cardboard boxes of cut flowers. The car smelled like a perfumery.

'Very feminine,' said Jonas, inhaling. 'Nice. Now where?'

'Back to my flat. Natalya will be waiting with the van. We're going down to the church together.'

But Hope's phone beeped and there was a text from Natalya. 'Oh.'

'What is it?'

'She's got to collect the bridegroom's mother and take her down as well. She's already on her way. She's told me to take a cab.'

314

'Where to?'

They were sitting at traffic lights. Even this early, traffic was building up in the main entry roads to London.

'The Surrey hills somewhere. Natalya's got the directions.' Hope was busy trying to text as the car started to move again.

'Have you got the postcode?'

'Yes. It's the church. It's on all the invitations. Why?'

'Because I have this car, this car has satnav. We don't need Natalya's directions.'

She was taken aback. 'You can't drive me all that way. There and back, unloading . . . it would take the whole morning!'

'It's Friday. Our Most Difficult Client plays golf every Friday. Anyone else can wait.'

'And I have to go back to the flat first. I've got stuff to take and a weekend suitcase for me.'

'No problem. I'll tell the office to expect me when they see me.'

'You'd really do that?'

He gave her one of his special smiles,

slow and deep and full of affection. If she let it, her whole body would smile right back. That didn't feel as alarming as it would have done a week ago. She still didn't let it happen. But she stretched a little in her seat, looking at the London street curling its way between shops and office blocks ahead of them, and explored this new calm. She liked it.

'For you? Anything.' It sounded as if he really meant it.

Hope was suddenly breathless. She kept her eyes on the windscreen. 'Then it really is my lucky day.'

It was meant to be a joke. But as soon as she said it, it felt like the truth.

★   ★   ★

It was a long, sprawling village, but Jonas found the church easily enough. He even managed to park in the curve of an ancient wall. The church itself was locked.

So Hope went to find the key while

he transferred all the flower boxes into the shadowed porch. It took a while. He enjoyed it. It felt good to be working in tandem with Hope again. He realized how much he'd missed it. In those short few weeks in the San Michele forest he'd become so used to it, it felt as if they had always been a team.

He finished unloading before she returned. So he leaned against the side of the car and consulted his messages. The rental agreement had come through. He scanned it quickly, supplied an automated signature, transferred the required deposit and a month's rent in advance, and set up a direct debit for subsequent months while he waited.

He wondered whether he'd manage to persuade her to visit him there. She'd backed away last night and he'd thought that meant no chance. But today she seemed more . . . accepting, somehow. Even relaxed, as she used to be.

Of course, that could change again. Well, it was just up to him to make sure it didn't. So that was what he would do, every opportunity that he got.

He folded his arms and gave himself up to happy contemplation of a fine oak and an ancient yew in the churchyard. He was watching a couple of starlings squabbling, their feathers iridescent in the morning sun, when she came back with the key and two coffees.

'Sorry I was so long. Got passed from hand to hand. Natalya isn't here yet.' She handed over one of the paper cups. 'Fortunately the post office is open and does the essentials. You were looking very peaceful.'

He nodded. 'It's a peaceful place.'

She laughed. 'You should see it this afternoon when all the main players descend.'

He sipped his coffee. 'I can do that. If it would help.'

She shook her head decisively. 'Kind of you, but no thanks. This is my job. Besides, you've got a rental agreement to sign and a flat to move into.'

'Signed and paid for. Did it while I

was waiting. As for moving in — it's only a couple of suitcases. I'll need to think about how to make it less impersonal. Any suggestions?'

But she wasn't to be drawn on that, he saw. Not yet, at least. And, anyway, she was itching to get back to those flowers.

So he abandoned his own project and said, 'Right, let's get your flowers into the church. And where do you want me to take your suitcase?'

'Oh, don't bother, I'll take it up later.'

But they hadn't finished moving half the flowers before the advance guard of village flower arrangers arrived.

'They're early,' said Hope, half-laughing, half-dismayed.

'They're just keen.'

'I wish Natalya were here. I've got the plan for the flower arrangements, but she's the one who's been dealing with it.'

She looked so worried that he wanted to hug her and tell her she would be fine. *Not yet*, he reminded himself. *Not until I'm sure she wants me to.* 'Look, you're going to have your hands full. I'll just take your stuff up to wherever you're staying and get out of your hair.'

Hope looked harassed. But in the end, she didn't take much convincing. She gave him the address of the B&B and sent him off with a hurried wave as she disappeared into the posse of flower arrangers.

Jonas delivered the suitcase and a couple of bags and then drove quietly back to London. For the first time since that vile vintage ball, he felt that he'd done something right.

He realized that he'd been thinking so much about the big dramatic moments in their relationship — when he was generally making a major mess of things, to be fair — that he had forgotten that gentle intimacy when they were just doing stuff together. He'd followed Hope to England, with no real strategy, just knowing that it wasn't over.

But now he thought, *Did I think I could get that life in a bubble back? What an idiot!* Fantasy time was over. And he was glad.

Now he knew what he wanted, no question about it. No doubts, no reservations. He wanted to be there for Hope and he wanted her to know it. Oh, he wanted more than that, of course he did. But first and foremost, he wanted to be her go-to guy for the big stuff and the little, in good times and bad.

It was as simple as that. Jonas was astonished.

He wanted to be her guy. For always.

13

Hope was in the church, dogsbodying for the flower ladies, when Natalya arrived.

'Really sorry to let you down like that.' It sounded as if Natalya was hanging on to her temper by a thread. 'How on earth did you get all those flowers down here?'

'I had help.' Hope could feel herself blushing, though there was absolutely no reason for it. She ignored it and hoped Natalya didn't notice. 'I know a man with a car and an early-morning exercise habit. He just cut the jog and drove me down here instead.'

'Thank the Lord. I suppose he's not available tomorrow, too?'

Hope laughed. But later, in conference with Cindy, it was clear that Natalya had not been entirely joking.

'We're going to be really pressed

when people start arriving this evening. In my view, the bridegroom's mother is going to need a minder at all times.'

'What?' Hope was horrified. She knew just how tight the timetable was, and it was already beginning to drift.

Cindy stayed calm. 'I was afraid of that. It's the first time she'll be on her own at a big function since her husband left, poor woman. She's been compensating by helping.'

'Interfering,' muttered Natalya.

'Trying to help,' allowed Cindy. 'But she won't have a role from now on. We'll need a rota so she's always got someone in hand-holding distance if she feels a wobbly coming on. The ushers will help out.'

But after the wedding rehearsal that evening, it became clear that the ushers were not a reliable source of assistance.

'A flake and a geek and two husbands,' said Natalya in despair. 'Any chance of calling in your jogger, Hope?'

Hope's stomach dropped sixty floors in two seconds, picked itself up, did a double somersault and then shot off into space whistling a merry tune. 'He did offer,' she admitted. 'I suppose I could call him.'

She did, apologetically. 'I know you're moving in this weekend. But if you could spare a couple of hours . . . '

'I'll be down tonight.'

'What?'

'It'll take me an hour and a half, tops. I'll take my suitcases round to the new apartment and come straight from there. Say nine o'clock. Where shall I find you? At the B&B?'

'No. There's a pre-wedding buffet supper for friends and relations who have had to travel. It's at the hotel where a lot of them are staying.' She gave him the address. 'I'll keep some food for you.'

She reported her success. 'He'll need a room for the night.'

Natalya began, 'Won't he share your . . . ?' but a look from Cindy shut her up.

'I'll get him a room at the hotel,' Cindy said firmly. 'What's his name?'

'Jonas Reval,' said Hope without thinking.

Cindy wrote it down, then looked at it. 'How do you spell that?'

Too late, Hope remembered — Cindy had been a diplomat's wife. Unlike Hope, she'd probably recognize the name at once. Still, there was nothing else to do but spell it out. She did, and held her breath.

But all Cindy said was, 'Fine. Leave it with me.' But her eyes were sharp.

* * *

When Jonas arrived, Hope was prowling in the gardens outside the main entrance. Waiting for him? He couldn't be sure. She was frowning and clutching a clipboard. She didn't look up as he drove past.

He parked and went over to her. 'Hi.'

She jumped and swung round. 'Jonas. Oh, thank heavens.' He could see she looked frantic, unless it was a trick of the summer twilight.

'What's up?'

It poured out in sort of breathless gabble. He understood that she had betrayed him, that she'd put him in danger and that the gods were attacking her with thunderbolts. None of which seemed likely or, indeed, possible.

'Hey,' he said, as she showed no sign of either clarifying or falling silent. 'I'm lost. What's the problem? Don't you want me after all?'

For a moment he thought she would actually cry. Then she swallowed and said, 'Breathe, Hope. Breathe.'

'I think that should be my line,' he said, amused. 'Do you want me to go away again? Or shall we go to wherever I'm staying? And then we can talk about whatever's bothering you.'

'No.' It was halfway to a scream. She caught herself and did some more careful breathing. 'I mean neither. The thing is, you're staying here.'

'Great. I'll check in, then.'

She moaned. 'That's the trouble. You're registered here as Jason Rebel.'

'What?'

'It was my fault. Cindy asked me what your name was and I said . . . '

Jonas began to laugh. 'You were economical with the truth? You? I'm shocked,' he said when he could speak.

She pushed a harassed hand through her hair. 'I deserve that,' she said ruefully. 'But no, I wasn't. Well, not exactly. I said you were Jonas Reval all right. But then . . . '

He wanted to hug her. 'You overlooked my dignities and titles. It's easily done. I forgive you.'

She met his eyes and flushed faintly. 'You have every right to rub it in,' she conceded.

He did hug her then, though quite lightly.

'Don't beat yourself up about it. I kept you in the dark for much too long.'

She gave his arm a grateful squeeze. 'But if the hotel knows who I am, I don't understand the need for a *nom de guerre*.'

'The hotel doesn't know. It's my Aunt

Cindy. She was making up a rota and that's the name she put on it. Jason Rebel.'

'She's dyslexic?'

'She's an operator,' said Hope sourly. She was recovering by the minute. 'I've only just found out. She knows who you are. She recognized the name and then she did a Google search, to be sure.'

'Most people do,' he said comfortingly. He put his arm round her waist. 'Come on, it's not the end of the world. Actually, it's funny if you look at it the right way. I take it I'm Jason for the duration? To everyone?'

'Yes. And she said people will be taking lots of pictures to post on the bride and groom's website. So avoid cameras if you can.'

He pulled a face. 'Been doing that all my life. Not a problem.'

She stared. 'All your life?'

'I'll tell you about it sometime. Is that it?'

Hope nodded.

'Then let's go.'

The hotel reception didn't need a credit card, as his room would go on the wedding planners' bill but they asked for his driving licence or passport. It was only what Jonas expected, after Hope's revelation. He patted his pockets convincingly and then discovered that he'd left his driving licence behind when he hired the car. 'It was all such a rush,' he explained.

Well, the hotel, who had been asked for the room less than two hours before, already knew that. The receptionist was sympathetic.

'And I did make a note of the car registration number for your car park attendant.' He handed across a scrubby bit of paper.

The receptionist decided that he was well-meaning but a bit thick. She smiled forgivingly, gave him a key card and wished him a successful stay.

'You're very plausible.' Hope accompanied him to the lift, clipboard in hand.

The poor darling was clearly torn.

The upright citizen in her obviously felt that she should deplore the practised ease of his deception. But she was a realist and she must be only too aware that she was in no position to take the moral high ground, since he was lying at her instigation.

'Must be tough,' he sympathized.

'What?' Hope looked at him with suspicion.

'Being an accessory before the fact.'

She snorted. 'Blasted lawyer!' But he could see that she was having to fight down laughter.

His heart lifted. 'Just doing my best,' he said, mock-injured.

She did laugh then. 'Stop winding me up, you!'

She peered at the little envelope containing his key card and made a note of the number before giving him an envelope from the boss woman.

'That's the running order for tonight and tomorrow plus maps of the village and the venues. There's a meeting in Cindy's room after dinner this evening.

Details are all in there. Come down to the garden room and eat when you're ready.'

The buffet supper was good, and the thirty or so guests seemed to be getting along together fine, sitting at a couple of long tables. Jonas was used to a whole range of events and recognized the meticulous organization that had gone into making a disparate group of strangers feel this comfortable with each other.

'I'm impressed,' he told Hope as they said goodnight before she and Natalya went back to their B&B in the village.

She chuckled. 'Don't sound so surprised.'

'I'm not. You'd make a success of anything you choose to do. You pay attention.'

Hope looked astonished, then endearingly confused by the compliment. 'I just do what I'm told. I'm working for experts,' she said gruffly, and hurried off into the dark — probably in case he tried to kiss her, Jonas thought, disappointed.

He found her Aunt Cindy looking at him beadily. He raised an eyebrow, challenging her to comment. But she just wished him good night and hurried off.

*   *   *

The wedding went off perfectly. Hope could hardly believe it. Even the temperamental mother of the bridegroom had a good time. She turned out to be a talented dancer, once Jonas had persuaded her onto the dance floor. Thereafter she danced with all her son's friends and several of her own generation as well, and finally left with an airy wave in the direction of her ex-husband. For Hope it was the crowning triumph of an extraordinary weekend.

'How did you do that?' Hope asked him over an early breakfast next day, marvelling.

'Dancing is chapter three of the prince's handbook. My grandmother started me on lessons when I was eight.'

'Yes, but she was so jumpy about meeting new people! I never dreamed she'd come out from behind the flower arrangements and dance.'

Jonas pulled a face. 'That's chapter one. "Your job is to ensure that people feel they have been recognized and respected as individuals."' He was clearly quoting. The self-mockery was evident.

She frowned. 'But you didn't just make her feel respected. You gave her confidence. No, more than that. You made her feel that if she did get the dance wrong, it would just add to the fun, somehow.'

He shrugged. 'Same thing.'

'I don't think so.'

But he brushed it aside. 'What do we have to do today?'

'Just take the flower boxes to the recycling collection point. Preferably getting them out of the vestry before the family service at eleven o'clock. If that's OK?'

He grinned. 'I'm awake. You're

awake. The conservationist in me is dancing a jig with delight. Very much OK, I'd say.'

She'd thought it would take hours, but he made short work of the pile, even though it had filled half the church vestry. He ripped open the thickly glued corners that she and the flower ladies had struggled with in vain on Friday, and then flattened and folded the stiff cardboard as if it were newspaper.

'Jump on that,' he invited as he began to build a pile. 'This stuff fights back.'

Choirboys, arriving for the morning service, joined in too. Even the vicar took an experimental bounce or two, at Jonas's suggestion.

'Great team work here,' said Jonas, smiling at Hope.

She found herself smiling back, happy. Working together again filled her with an overwhelming sense of rightness. Jonas too, if she was any judge.

He drove her back to London via the recycling bank. They were so close, their shoulders almost touching, that she couldn't help remembering San Michele. She sighed.

Jonas sent her a quick look. 'Glad it's over?'

'Glad it went well,' she corrected.

'Does it get to you, though? Wedding organization looked like a high-anxiety activity to me.'

'You plan as much as you can, and prepare for things to go wrong. There's always something. I quite enjoy that aspect of it.'

'Yes, I can see that you would. All those different jobs. You've got a lot of experience to draw on.'

Hope considered. 'I suppose you're right. And I'm good in a crisis.'

'I remember.' He looked serious. He said suddenly, 'Do you still want to duck whenever anyone points a camera at you?'

Hope was startled. 'Did I say that?'

'Yes. You looked really sick when you talked about it. That's why — ' He broke off.

Hope was intrigued. 'Why what?'

Jonas said uncomfortably, 'Why I vetoed Klaus naming you in the rangers' report on the rescue.'

'You vetoed it? But you said . . . '

'I know what I said. Another instance of me telling you less than the truth, I'm afraid.'

She was shaken. 'Did I ask you to? I don't remember.'

'No,' he said swiftly. 'No, it was all my idea. It was obvious that the press release worried you. You didn't deserve to be worried. You'd done enough, going down that rope. So I pulled rank and said we keep the prince and the prince's girlfriend out of the story.'

Prince's girlfriend? 'Oh.'

'And then afterwards, when you told me about people spitting at you in the street . . . ' His hands clenched on the wheel. 'I'd do it again,' he said fiercely.

Girlfriend. Really?

'Dealing with the press is something I've done all my life. Unlike you, I've never had to face actual hostility. They've always been rather kind. But I know them. They don't let up. Give them a story and they have to dig. Even if Klaus had just said that a member of the public helped with the rescue, it wouldn't have kept you out of the story for long. Some journalist would have identified you. Then they'd have got to your father and what he did. Then they'd have had a story.' He sounded weary. 'It wasn't fair.'

'I didn't realize.' Hope was still wrestling with the fact that he called her his girlfriend. As if it was accepted fact.

'You weren't supposed to.'

She burst out, 'Why did you tell Klaus I was your girlfriend?'

'What?' He sounded utterly blank.

She repeated it.

He cast her a quick look of disbelief. 'You're joking, right? I didn't have to *tell* Klaus. The rangers could all see how hard I'd fallen for you. And we were meeting every day. For heaven's sake, it was obvious.'

'Not to me.'

They were coming off the motorway and into London traffic. Jonas said in evident desperation, 'I can't have this conversation and drive properly. Come back with me to the flat.'

Hope jumped in her seat as if he had stuck a needle into her spine. An ice-cold needle. Her mouth dried. She knew she could say no, insist on going back to her own place, close the door on him and regroup her defences. Half of her wanted to. But the other half, the one that had taken her travelling in the first place and knew that there was no peace until you turned and faced your demons, said, *This is it, then.*

'All right,' she said faintly. She had never felt so scared in her life.

*   *   *

Jonas was a realist, he told himself. He knew that Hope agreeing to come home with him was not a full declaration of trust. But he still treasured the memory of Hope's undisguised joy when she

338

caught sight of him in Green Park. And now they were talking properly, too.

It was progress. Not a whole new start. But progress, nevertheless. So he had to go carefully, he thought. Stick to practicalities. No emotional pressure.

He said, 'I haven't moved in properly. I can't even give you a cup of coffee until I've picked up the basics.'

'There's a big supermarket coming up,' Hope suggested. 'We can park and shop.'

They did. They went round like a couple of students, tossing whatever took their fancy into the shopping trolley. Jonas bought coffee, pasta, wine, a wide selection from the delicatessen counter and a kaleidoscope of cheeses. Hope bought salad, bread, milk and tea. And a lot of cleaning materials. They eyed each other's choices at the checkout. Jonas raised an eyebrow.

'You'll need washing-up liquid,' said Hope defensively. 'And I bet you haven't got tea towels.' They had both bought candles.

Their eyes met. Jonas couldn't help himself. He began to laugh. Hope smiled reluctantly. Then succumbed.

'Oh, how ridiculous,' she gasped, holding her side. 'Don't make me laugh any more. It hurts.'

But when they were back in the car, Jonas started again. 'You know what Nico would say? Nice try, but next time be more lavish.'

Hope mopped her eyes. 'Your brother Nico?'

'My heartthrob brother. He's big on romantic gestures. Soft music, dancing by starlight under palm trees on a tropical beach.'

Hope sniffed. 'Sounds like an advert for middle-market chocolates.'

Jonas looked at her affectionately. He nearly said that he knew exactly what her romantic idyll involved — a makeshift bed on the floor, a blazing fire and a night of thunder and lightning outside. Maybe not yet, he thought. And oh the morning, with her tousled hair, the covers slipping off her shoulder and her eyes full of the night's delights, as she teased him and ate apple crumble for breakfast! He shifted sharply. This was *not* a productive line of thought at this stage. Rewarding though. His lips twitched.

He turned the engine on. 'Last leg. Let's go home.'

The really odd thing was that Hope did treat the empty apartment as if it were home. The moment he let them into the entrance hall, she was looking round as if she were taking mental notes. She quartered the floor space like a general.

'Plenty of light, nice layout, bit bland. Needs cushions. But that's OK, you get to pick your own colours.'

'When I get round to it, maybe.' Jonas began to unpack their shopping.

Hope sat on the smart leather sofa and kicked off her shoes, tucking her feet under her. 'It's nice having a blank canvas. I'm really house-sitting rather than renting, so I'm surrounded by someone else's collected life.'

She sounds wistful, he thought.

341

'Surely you're used to that, travelling as you do? The Antons' villa must have been the same.'

'Yes,' she agreed at once. 'Of course, you're right. Or maybe I'm just tired of perching and want to nest-build.'

'So why don't you?'

He saw her jump, as if she had suddenly realized what she had said and wished she hadn't. After a fractional pause she said, 'My parents weren't really homemakers. So no role model.'

He surprised himself by saying, 'I suppose I'm the same, in a way.' He looked at the packet of ground coffee in his hands, turning it over and over. 'When I came to the villa and you made me supper, I used to think that must be what coming home would feel like.'

Hope stilled, staring at him. 'But you must have done it. Lots of times. Come home I mean.'

He shook his head. 'It was all airports and officials and updating engagement diaries. My friend Jack from Iowa State pointed out to me once that I never said, 'I'm going home for Christmas.' I always said, 'I'm going to San Michele on the 23rd.''

She absorbed that. 'But your apartment in Liburno. Isn't that your home these days?'

'Until we met, I suppose I would have said that it was, yes. But now — no, I don't think so. It's more of a den. I don't invite people there. I've never shared it.'

She looked at him beadily. 'You certainly never invited me there.'

He stopped kneading the packet of coffee in simple amazement. 'Is that a joke?'

'What? No, of course not.'

Jonas said with a restraint he was proud of, 'When I did, you turned me down flat and accused me of having no respect for you or your job.'

Hope's eyes widened. 'What?'

His restraint slipped a bit. 'I damn nearly *begged* you to come with me.'

She jumped up, agitated, and began to prowl about the room. 'Oh, that's awful. I just thought you were being high-handed.'

He watched her. 'Do you want to know something really crazy? It didn't feel right being there on my own. I really missed you.'

She shook her head, still agitated. 'I didn't *know*. I'm so sorry.'

'In fact, I promised myself I'd tell you everything when I came back. Ask you to stay on in San Michele when your job with the Antons ended.' He hesitated, not sure whether this was the right time. But then it surged out of him anyway. 'Maybe live with me, if you could face the gossip.'

She gave a low cry, as if she'd burned herself. '*We need to talk*,' she hissed, still striding. 'Stupid, stupid, *stupid*!'

Jonas was confused. 'You've lost me.'

Hope rounded on him. Her eyes glittered. 'You sent me a text. *We need to talk*.'

She sounded furious. That confused him even more. 'Did I?'

'Yes, you did. Why did you think I

was so crazy that night at dinner?'

He spread his hands, looking a question.

'Because of that text.'

'Huh?'

'It's the classic this-is-only-a-holiday-fling text. I thought you were signing me off.'

Jonas winced. It sounded really ugly. And then he thought back to that evening. Her explosion. The profound closeness of those moments on the bridge. The night that followed. And he wasn't confused anymore. 'No you didn't,' he said positively. 'Not after that night.'

That stopped her. She rounded on him and for a second he thought she was going to flame him. But then her shoulders fell and she blinked rapidly.

'Maybe,' she said distantly. 'But the whole of that day. Waiting for the axe to fall. It shook me. It really shook me.' She turned her back and fumbled with the catch to the great windows that led out onto roof terrace. Her shoulders were shaking.

Jonas wondered for a horrible moment whether it was with silent laughter at the cruel irony of the misunderstanding. But then he looked more closely and realized that it was a sort of dreadful silent sobbing that Hope didn't want him to see.

He followed her. She was standing under the shade of one of the tubbed birch trees. She didn't turn round.

Jonas said quietly, 'I knew I was falling in love with you from the day we met.'

She just shook her head, not turning to face him.

He stepped out onto the terrace but didn't touch her. 'Sometimes I thought you were, too. I was never sure. But after that night, I thought the only problem was how busy you were with the Antons' child.'

'It didn't occur to you to tell me who you were, though, did it?' She swung round, glaring at him. 'Be honest with me.'

It was so unexpected that he spoke

without thinking. 'Oh for heaven's sake, are we back on the prince thing again? How many times do I have to say it? I *never* lied to you.'

'That is *such* a lawyer's answer,' she said with contempt.

'What the hell do you mean by that?'

'Remember the evidence oath?' she taunted him. 'The truth, the whole truth and nothing but the truth? You may not have resorted to out-and-out falsehood. But you sure as hell never told me the whole truth.'

He flung up his hands in a despairing gesture. 'What can I say? When I saw you at the chateau, I couldn't believe my luck. If you'd just listened to me instead of racing off round those statues and disappearing — '

Hope took a hasty step forward. 'Don't you patronize me,' she yelled. 'What good would it have done to listen to you? I didn't have a lie detector in my purse.'

She was close enough to kiss. Jonas held on to his sanity with heroic resolution. 'I'm sorry. I didn't mean to sound patronizing.'

'Well, you did. Thoroughly princely, in fact.'

He saw that she was being nasty in pure self-defence. All desire to defend himself evaporated. 'That's a low blow. And I probably deserve it. I'm sorry, love.'

'Don't you dare be nice to me.'

'I only meant that I could have explained.'

'Explained? I don't think so. Can you deny that there was a moment when you knew you ought to tell me you were a San Michele prince and you decided not to?'

He opened his mouth to deny it. Then he remembered that split-second decision in the forest. She'd just apologized handsomely for being grumpy, and she was starting to tease him and he couldn't bear to spoil it.

'See, you *can't*.' She didn't sound triumphant. All the fight seemed to have gone out of her. He wanted to hug her so badly it hurt.

'I'd forgotten,' he said at last.

'Even at the time, I knew there was *something*.' She sounded sad. 'I've developed these very good antennae for half-truths over the years. But I didn't want to believe it. So I decided to trust you. It's always a mistake to ignore my instincts.'

It found its mark like a stiletto. Jonas recoiled. He was silent for a long time. At last he said, 'In mitigation, my bossy sister-in-law had just been parading me in front of a bunch of film people. She had me all dressed up like a major general — sword, uniform and all. Making everyone call me Serene Highness. It was vile. When we met, I remember thinking thank God there are no Serene Highnesses in the forest.'

She didn't laugh. Didn't even smile. Jonas couldn't blame her. She'd decided to trust him and she'd made the wrong call. He was never coming back from that. 'But you're right. I admit it. I made a choice. The wrong one.'

Hope made a helpless gesture. 'I'm sorry too.'

She went back indoors and he watched helplessly as she searched for her shoulderbag. When she found it, she turned with that polite social smile that he dreaded and said, 'Thank you for all your help this weekend. It was kind of you.'

He couldn't bear it. He said, 'Marry me.'

He might as well have threatened her with a lightsabre. Hope sent him one appalled look and fled.

14

Hope walked home. She was too wired to sit in a bus or even a taxi.

I knew I was falling in love with you from the day we met.

How could she believe him? He'd never said anything about love.

She made herself a meal but then couldn't face eating. After a mouthful or two it went in the bin. 'I'm missing Moby,' she said aloud. And started to laugh. It sounded more like crying.

She thought of calling Ally. But Ally had her own problems and hadn't been in touch for weeks. Besides, Ally already thought Hope and Jonas had unfinished business. She'd just tell Hope to deal with it.

She went to bed. Didn't sleep. Tried reading, TV, radio. Nothing worked. By dawn her face in the bathroom mirror was haggard. Her mother would have said she was bottling things up and needed to break something. Hope smiled reluctantly. *Good thinking, Mama.* Only she couldn't break someone else's china. And if she wanted to scream, she'd better go home and find a quiet corner of the grounds at Hasebury Hall where no one would hear.

She was looking up the timetable on her phone when a text came through. It was from Jonas. Her heart lurched. She nearly deleted it unopened. But her mother's words echoed. 'Sticking your head in the sand never works, darling.'

It read: *I still have your bags. Can I bring them round?* He had sent it five minutes ago. Outside it was barely light. Had his night been as sleepless as hers, then?

Before she could talk herself out of it, she texted back: *Yes. Come now.* Though she hadn't a clue what she was going to say to him.

He looked rough, with shadows like bruises under his eyes. Hope's heart went out to him. 'You need your forest badly.'

He put down her overnight case and the other bags. 'You're looking pretty ragged yourself. Bad night?'

'Yup.'

He closed his eyes briefly. 'Look, I'm sorry. I never meant to unload all that stuff on you yesterday.'

There it was again. *I knew I was falling in love with you from the day we met.* Hope swallowed. 'Did you mean it?'

'Oh yes.'

Not just the words; his whole body said it was true. She couldn't *not* believe him when he looked like that. It was like a punch to the gut. Hope sat down hard. She felt horrible, sitting on the edge of the seat, twisting her hands as she struggled to find words to explain something she didn't understand herself. She said haltingly, 'When we met, my first instinct was to walk away.'

'I remember.'

'But I wanted to see you again, do you see? So I ignored my instinct. Only it was right, wasn't it?'

Jonas sank down slowly onto the sofa opposite. Hope couldn't look at him. But she knew his eyes didn't leave her face.

'If I'd googled you or something sensible like that, I'd have found out everything right then.' The self-mockery was bitter. 'But I was determined to trust, for once in my life. And then, at the chateau, when I found out the truth about you, I thought, serves me right.'

There was a long silence. Then Jonas said carefully, 'And now?'

She pushed her hands through her hair. 'I seem to have two sets of instincts, and they're at war.'

Hope was shaking with cold, though the morning sun was warm on her shoulders. She wished Jonas would put his arms round her and hold her close. But she knew that if he tried to, she would push him away, and not kindly. 'I think I'm going crazy,' she muttered.

She clutched her arms round herself and tried to still the trembling.

Eventually Jonas said, 'May I suggest something?'

Hope nodded, not looking at him. 'Go ahead.'

'When we got together, you were in a new job in a new country and I was on holiday from my normal life. Agreed?'

'Yes.'

'So we didn't do most of the normal dating things people do when they're getting to know one another. So my suggestion is, we do that now.'

She looked at him then. 'We *date*?'

'Why not? We even both have relatively normal jobs at the moment.'

She saw an objection at once. 'But you work all week and I have to work every weekend.'

'Couples on shift work manage it. So can we.'

She was still doubtful. 'It would feel awkward.'

'Yes, probably. We'd get over it.' And when she still looked sceptical he said,

'At least it would give us a *chance*.'

He sounded desperate, Hope thought. She opened her mouth to say that it was hopeless. That she couldn't trust him again. But her heart whispered to her and she stumbled.

Unfinished business.

She said, 'Then you'll have to come on the wedding assignments with me. There's no way I can moonlight as a lawyer.'

And at last he smiled. 'It's a deal.'

★ ★ ★

It was a busy summer — for both of them.

Jonas had to travel all over the world for work, but he was at her side for at least some part of nearly every weekend wedding. He didn't make it to midweek ones, but he always texted to wish her luck and called to find out how it had gone.

She thought, *This is going to work.*

He gave her sweet, silly presents and

took her to his old haunts in Cambridge and London. Once he sent her flowers out of the blue, for no reason except that he wanted to say he loved her. Sometimes Hope felt as if she had been transported to an alternative universe where nothing was quite real. She kept expecting to wake up.

She told him so, laughing. 'You should write the Perfect Boyfriend's Handbook.'

But he shook his head, serious. 'I'm still learning.'

Their sexual attraction simmered, tacitly acknowledged but never quite brought into the light. Jonas drove her home, kissed her goodnight and scrupulously left her at the front steps to her house.

Once, under the influence of a long slow dance under the stars on his terrace, Hope kissed him with all the old passion. He caught his breath and his hands grew urgent. But almost at once, the old doubts started whispering. In spite of herself, she tensed.

At once he let her go and put distance between them. 'Too soon,' he said. It wasn't a question.

She denied it ferociously. But the moment had passed. Jonas killed the music, brought her a glass of wine and persuaded her to sit on the sofa again while he took himself off to a bamboo chair. They talked a little, and when she finished her wine, he took her home.

When he stopped the car outside her house, he said in a strained voice, 'Hope, I really want to make love to you. But I won't until and unless you trust me. And neither of us can force it.'

That night the kiss was a gentle brush of the lips against her cheek. Perversely, she could have jumped his bones, given the slightest encouragement. She tossed and turned all night, frustrated and confused.

But the next day, Jonas was himself again practical and attentive. Sexy as hell.

Unattainable.

Except that he wasn't unattainable,

was he? All she had to do was learn to trust him. But *how*?

As summer turned into autumn, Hope lurched from one extreme to the other. Jonas remained steady, a rock during the frequent wedding crises, kind and funny always. But that slight distance he had set between them didn't diminish. Hope missed their former closeness and knew she had only herself to blame.

Then, at the younger generation's party after a sedate suburban wedding, the DJ failed to turn up, and Jonas had turned out to be an inspired substitute. When the party finally wound to a close, there was a roar of approval. Jonas grinned and bowed like a pro. Hope wanted to give him a congratulatory hug so much that it was a physical pain.

Under cover of the cheering, Cindy said, 'Hope, are you exploiting that young man?'

Hope was startled. 'What do you mean?'

Cindy said carefully, 'Hope dear, it's

clear that something's wrong. I know a relationship with royalty is never easy. But you can't just keep him on a string. It isn't fair.'

It was a shock. 'I'm not. Am I? I mean — I never meant to.'

Cindy nodded. 'I understand. Things happen and then you find you've fallen into a pattern and you can't get out of it. But there's only so many times you can push someone away, sweetie. I've done it.'

Hope was silenced. She put her arm round her aunt.

Cindy's back was ramrod straight, but her shoulders softened a little at the embrace. She opened her eyes very wide and didn't take them off the departing dancers at their farewells.

'You're a sensible young woman,' she said at last. 'Much more mature than I was at your age. And brave, too. Now you just need to be brave about this relationship and make up your mind.' She patted Hope's arm. 'I have faith in you.'

Hope helped with the clearing up but with only half her mind engaged.

Be brave.

Was it as simple as that? Just make up her mind, like deciding which country to visit, and go for it?

And then it struck her. Maybe it wasn't Jonas that she couldn't bring herself to trust. Maybe it was herself.

Jonas drove her back, as always. The roads were empty. It was nearly dawn by the time they reached London. Hope sat beside him, watching the attention he paid to the road, not letting the lack of traffic distract him. Relaxed, yet alert. Yes, that was Jonas. You felt he was competent to deal with anything without being a control freak or wanting to run the world.

She said slowly, 'I know you really well, don't I?'

He sent her a swift, startled look. But all he said was, 'Yes, I believe so.'

Later, when they came to the point where he should turn off to drive to her flat, he said, 'Are you tired?'

'No.' Because she wasn't. She was beyond tired and had reached a state of Zen acceptance. Oddly, it felt both peaceful and wildly exciting.

'Then come to breakfast. We can drink champagne on the terrace and watch the sunrise.'

Ah.

The moment of decision. Not this very minute, but heading towards her, inexorable as that sunrise.

And I'm ready. Bring it on.

'Yes,' she said.

But when they arrived, Jonas surprised her. 'Time may be running out on us, sweetheart. There was a question about you and me at the press round-up meeting on Friday.'

Hope stared. 'What press round-up meeting?'

'My sister-in-law has started a weekly meet-the-press gig.' It didn't sound as if he was a fan. 'Carlo texted me. One of the local journalists asked about a rumour that I was seeing someone in London.'

'Local? You mean in San Michele?'

'Yes, but the international circuit of royalty watchers will pick it up now. I'm sorry.'

Hope was puzzled. 'How is it your fault?'

His mouth twisted. 'Being a prince.'

'Oh. That.'

'I know the press gave you a bad time over your father's case.'

Hope shrugged. 'That was a long time ago.'

He studied her expression, looking arrested. 'But I thought . . . People spat at you. It sounded appalling.'

He looked so worried that Hope took his hand in both of hers. 'Not as appalling as having my father locked away in prison. It was nasty at the time. But I'm over it. Nobody's going to spit at me because I'm dating you, are they?'

Jonas looked down at their clasped hands. 'I thought that was half the problem. The risk of press intrusion.'

Hope shook her head. 'No.'

'I've dreaded the gossip columnists and the paparazzi. It's sort of inevitable and I knew — thought — they'd hurt you badly. I couldn't bear to bring all that up for you again.'

'I did tell you, I'm not a paparazzi victim. Maybe once, but I was very young and the situation was horrible. I've grown up since.'

He swallowed.

She swung their clasped hands gently. 'Look at me, Jonas.'

He did, scanning her expression.

'There are worse things in the world than gossip columns,' Hope said steadily. 'I can cope.'

He let out his breath in a great whoosh of astonished relief. 'So you can face the whole world knowing that you're dating a prince?'

She held his gaze. 'More than that.'

He grew very intent. 'Explain!'

The moment of choice, then. It was here. Hope disengaged her hand. She didn't know what to say.

Jonas had proposed to her in this

very room. But it had been a spur-of-the-moment thing. How could she be certain that his feelings weren't the result of a guilty conscience because he knew he'd hurt her? Half lust, half good manners, and wholly temporary!

Then she remembered their night in the forest hut. The way he'd got up to feed the fire and warmed her clothes for her in the morning. And her last fear winked out. Good manners, certainly. Lust, no question. But much, much more than that. And she'd recognized it too, back then. He might not have told her in words that he was falling in love with her. But he had shown her, again and again. She just hadn't understood.

Well, she did now. Hope felt as if she had come out of a suffocating fog. She said carefully, 'Do you remember telling me that you didn't have a concept of home?'

His eyes narrowed. 'I remember.'

'It wasn't true.'

That startled him. 'What do you mean?'

'Your concept of home is dodgy supper and a bed for the night in the Antons' villa. With me.'

The silence stretched between them as if time had stopped. At last Jonas cleared his throat. 'Yes. It is.'

She went back to him and put her hands on his shoulders, looking deeply into his eyes. 'I do trust you. I always have. I just . . . lost sight of it. Until now.'

He looked stunned. Then he said, as if he didn't quite believe it, 'Does that mean you'll marry me?'

'Yes.'

His arms went round her then. They were like a vice. He kissed her until she could hardly breathe.

When he raised his head, his face, his whole body, seemed alight. 'I had a very careful speech prepared. In fact several alternatives. All wasted.' He sounded gleeful as he felt in his pocket and brought out a small laminated envelope. He dropped its contents into his palm and looked up at her. 'I found this and thought of you. Was I right?'

He held it out to her. Hope stared, utterly silenced. It was a simple ring, a single stone, faceted and glowing with lights of spring leaf and young shoots, alternating with cosmic darkness. It was like looking into a forest lake, full of mystery. It would be like wearing their forest closeness on her hand.

'You were right,' she said, hardly above a whisper. She held out her hand and he slid it onto her finger. He kissed the back of her hand, then her palm, and then gathered her into his embrace.

'This,' he said with satisfaction, 'is going to be one spectacular sunrise.'

She jumped. He was right. The sky had already lightened considerably. There were streaks of lemon and apricot behind the cityscape.

'Are we going onto the terrace to watch it?'

'Do you want to?'

'Yes.'

But he brought her his thick coat and dropped it round her shoulders before he would let them go out into the autumnal dawn. They stood by the parapet as the horizon turned gold, he with his arm protectively around her shoulders, she with her right hand in his jacket pocket to keep warm, and her left enclosed in his own. They had never felt so close.

'I love my ring,' she murmured. 'What is it? I've never seen anything like it.'

He kissed her hair. 'Nor me. It's called a chrome tourmaline, apparently. I started looking for a ring that day you didn't come into Liburno with me. I knew it had to be special. I found this ring in an exhibition. It said Hope to me the moment I saw it.' He added ruefully, 'So I had to have it, even though I knew it might never be more than a souvenir of what might have been.'

Her heart turned over. 'Oh, love.'

He looked down at her. 'But I had no idea how much I had to learn.' He held her hand against his lips as if he would inhale her. 'I still can't quite believe you said yes.'

Hope thought her heart would burst. She wrapped her arms round him and said fiercely, 'Take me to bed. Now, please.'

He did.

15

Jonas insisted that the first thing they needed to do was tell their friends and family that they were engaged.

'Not that my father will be surprised. I told him last week that I was going to try to persuade you. Formally I need his permission.'

'He might say no.' Hope was teasing but his reaction startled her.

Jonas grinned evilly. 'Got it covered. He either says yes and I stay a prince, or he says no, I duck out of the succession, and you don't have to worry about being a Serene Highness.'

'You're joking.' But she saw that he wasn't. 'I think I may be out of my depth in the royalty department,' she murmured.

'Stick with me, babe. I've got your back.'

But the hereditary prince sent her a

handwritten note welcoming her to the family and inviting her to make an extended stay in the palace before the formal announcement of the engagement. He suggested they did that at Jonas's birthday ball on February 14th.

'That's because it's already in the diary,' said Jonas. 'Fine by me. What about you?'

'Do I have to hide my lovely ring until then?'

He hugged her. 'Never unless you want to.'

The crown princess also wrote, suggesting dates when Liburno Cathedral was available for a royal wedding and promising to brief Hope on protocol, court etiquette, royal obligations, important charities and local customs, including national dances.

'It sounds like a degree course,' said Hope faintly. She didn't say that she'd always thought she would marry in the village church, as her ancestors did.

But Jonas looked at her shrewdly. 'Bride gets to choose where she marries,' he said crisply. 'The interfering woman's not going to make your life a misery. You want to marry from Hasebury Hall and walk to that church, don't you?' Her eyes widened. He touched her face gently. 'I'll see her off. Should have done it long ago. We marry wherever you're happiest.'

Her eyes misted. 'Love you so much.'

And Jonas made love to her with dedicated skill, affection and just enough humour to save her from drowning.

Jonas had to travel nearly all the time now. They talked every day, though, and in London they spent all their free time together.

Hope began to find his cufflinks on her nightstand after black tie outings. And when he left early to fly to Copenhagen or Rome or Beijing, she would find little notes he'd left for her on the kitchen counter. They all ended the same. 'Still learning. Love you. J.'

Still, Hope had to go to Combe St Philip alone to deliver her news. She was touched by how pleased Max was at the decision and overwhelmed by the exuberant rejoicing of Flora and Ally, especially as Ally was back living with her parents in Combe St Philip, having lost her job on *Celebrity* magazine.

They had a girls' celebration picnic in front of the log fire in the shabby old library one evening and toasted the engagement.

'Our friend the princess.'

Hope pulled a face and shared the crown princess's suggested training programme. By the time she got to folk dancing, Flora was hugging her middle and moaning, 'No more, no more, my ribs hurt,' and Ally had got the hiccups from laughing.

It cheered Hope but she admitted, 'Jonas says ignore her but I think she may have a point. She's been doing the royal stuff for a long time. I'm going for a visit after Christmas.'

Ally and Flora looked at each other.

'Get everything important sorted before you go?' suggested Ally.

'There's Jonas, and Max and us too. Yay for Team Hope,' said Flora, raising a glass to solidarity.

'You and Jonas fix the date with St Philip's. I'll help with the press stuff. Heaven knows I've been doing it long enough. Flora will do the food.'

Flora nodded dreamily.

'You can organize your own wedding. You know how. Between us we can see off twenty crown princesses. Go us!'

Hope gave thanks for Team Hope regularly when she arrived in San Michele.

The palace turned out to be a mediaeval fortress with a Hapsburg ballroom extension that was twice as large as the original castle. Every staircase was grander than the last. Hope clocked two of marble and one of intricately carved oak within ten minutes of her arrival. And every room she entered seemed more gilded and glittering than the last.

Footmen in olive-green tail coats with gold brocade waistcoats led her through bewildering corridors every time she emerged from her room.

'I see what you mean about it not being very homely,' she told Jonas on their daily conversation. She tried to keep her side of the conversation light-hearted. The Difficult Client kept digging himself deeper and deeper into a hole, she could tell.

He laughed. 'Told you. We're soul-mates.'

She didn't tell him that the crown princess had uncovered Hope's fraud-ster father and, under the banner of helping a newbie, was becoming as difficult as the Client. But eventually Jonas sensed something. He arrived, unannounced, in the middle of an informal (only three footmen) family lunch in the tapestry-hung breakfast room.

'Just dropping in,' he said casually, throwing his briefcase onto a brocaded sofa and slipping into the seat next to Hope. 'On my way to Sydney this time.'

He kissed Hope's hand and held on

to it as a footman placed a plate of food in front of him. But when coffee was served and the footmen had retired, he stood up.

'Just wanted to get a few things clear.' Hope recognized steel behind his amiable smile and was taken aback. 'No press announcement or interview about our engagement goes out without referring to Hope. I'm in court too much at the moment to be reliable.'

The crown princess stiffened and folded her lips together in disapproval.

'This is not up for discussion,' said Jonas gently.

His father said, 'Quite right.'

'Thank you, Papa. And Hope and her team will deal with any enquiries about her family, particularly her father.' His eyes gleamed. 'As Papa has often pointed out, the Revals haven't been a hundred per cent respectable over the years. San Michele was founded as a pirate stronghold. A fraudster who paid his debt to society is small potatoes by comparison.'

There was a choke of laughter from

his rakehell brother Nico, and kind Carlo said, 'Hear, hear,' patting his wife's hand comfortingly.

'Am I clear?'

'Clear and very sensible,' said his father, sounding as if he meant it. 'Well done, Jonas.'

Hope texted the details to Ally and Flora after he'd gone for his flight. They were gleeful. The trouble was that it left the crown princess with responsibility for protocol, folk dancing and Hope's wardrobe.

For the next three weeks, Princess Anna threw herself into all of them with the enthusiasm of a frustrated mentor. She also found out about Hope's job with the Antons and her involvement with the forest rescue of the Boy Scout and determined that both could be usefully spun to the press.

Hope said no. Anna had to accept it, but she didn't do so easily or without planting several well-aimed barbs on Hope's lack of diplomacy or sense of responsibility.

Afterwards, Hope retired to bed before dinner with a favourite book. She felt as if she'd gone ten rounds with a prize fighter. She tried to call Jonas, but he was in a meeting.

She lay on top of the overstuffed duvet and brocaded coverlet, not reading, thoughts going round and round in her head.

I can't do this.

It will be fine when Jonas and I are together.

But will it? I can't do this for the rest of my life, being careful and diplomatic and never telling the truth about anything. I CAN'T.

It will be fine when Jonas is here.

But her confidence was shaken.

Jonas knew something was wrong and was desperate to get to Liburno to be with her. Contrarily, since that was all she really wanted, Hope told him to stay as long as he was needed. In the end, he got back just before Max and the girls were due to fly in.

'To meet the family before the ball,'

said Anna with one of the glittering smiles that didn't reach her eyes. 'And we've found you a beautiful dress.' She'd produced a folder of possible designs, each one more matronly than the one before.

Hope fled to her room.

This isn't like me. I've got to pull myself together.

She escaped for a couple of hours with kind Mrs Anton, who took her to a tiny boutique in Liburno where a young designer didn't expect formal clothes to look as if they had armoured corsets underneath. If only, thought Hope. But she reckoned she had pissed off the crown princess enough for one visit.

Jonas came back just in time for them both to go to the airport to meet the guests from England.

'Thank God for Team Hope,' she muttered, as they were driven across the tarmac to the plane. It felt as if it were the last time they would all be together.

She hid her feelings, though, and

even enjoyed introducing the English party to the ballroom with twenty-foot-high mirrors on every wall, four chandeliers, and a suite of sofas and chairs upholstered in gold brocade. The crown princess's programme was suffocatingly formal, but Ally and Flora organized a break-out to Liburno's club scene. Hope laughed and danced but was suddenly overwhelmed by a sense of impending loss. She slipped away before she started weeping.

Jonas found her on her own in the moonlight. 'I heard you took off. Regrets?'

She couldn't answer. She shook her head.

He seemed to take a decision. 'Then let's go.'

She looked round. 'I don't know where the others are . . . '

'No others,' said Jonas calmly. 'This is a kidnapping.'

'What?'

'As long as it's OK with you, of course.'

Hope stared, thinking of tomorrow's crowded programme. Three changes of clothes. Or was it four? 'Let's go,' she said.

'Right answer.' He took her hand and towed her round an eighteenth-century outcrop of palace.

She was shaken by a spurt of laughter.

He looked down at her. 'What?'

'It feels like bunking off behind the bike sheds,' said Hope, surprised into very un-royal spontaneous nonsense.

Jonas gave her a look that made her suddenly remember him saying *full-body kiss*. Her pulse started to race.

His fingers tightened painfully over hers. But all he said was, 'Glad you mentioned that. How do you feel about bikes?'

She wouldn't have cared if he'd said they were hiking to infinity. She was dancing inside. 'We're cycling?'

'A motorbike.'

And there it was, parked incongruously in front of a Corinthian column.

There were two helmets propped on top.

Hope stopped dead. 'We're running away to join the Hell's Angels!'

'Do you mind?'

'Mind? It's *wonderful*.'

'You'll be cold. Get some warm clothes on, gloves. Bring your passport.'

She did. They took off into the dawn.

He took her everywhere they'd been, she thought. They didn't mention family, or friends, or the wedding or anything that wasn't history or the natural world. Every time they got off the motorbike, they held hands and didn't let go. She felt the crown princess's corset giving up its grip, tie by suffocating tie.

Eventually Jonas took her hand and said, 'You've had a worse time than I realized. I'm sorry. Haven't learned enough about sharing essential information yet.' He squared his shoulders. 'So here's the thing. You have your passport. If you want to go home, I'll whip you over the border and you can fly home. I'll text Fredrik and he can tell everyone. No engagement announcement. No more wedding battles. You can be yourself again, my poor love.' He dropped her hand and stepped back.

Hope looked down at her engagement ring for a long moment. *Freedom*. Yesterday morning she had been so packed around with plans and diary events and moral obligations, it had seemed an unimaginable dream. And now he was offering it to her. As simply as a ride on a merry-go-round, as if it were nothing.

She looked up and caught his eyes on her, unaware. His face was naked with longing. And sadness. That was what caught her by the throat and stopped all her racing thoughts dead. *Sadness*. He wanted her. And he was saying goodbye. Because he thought she needed him to.

All the doubt of the last weeks flickered and went out. She knew what she wanted. She knew it was right. She knew it was the best thing for them both. She put her arms round him and said, 'But I want everyone to know we're engaged. I want to marry you. I can cope with the battles.'

He stared at her, clearly torn. How could she convince him? 'I still haven't seen your flat, Jonas. Let's go back to Liburno and make love.'

They did.

Afterwards, she soaked in a scented bath. Jonas wandered in and out, bringing her tea, then champagne, interspersed with plans for the future — chief among them *not* living in the palace, ever, on which they were as one — and news from the castle.

'I'll go back this evening though. I have to change for your birthday ball, anyway. You're not going to like my dress,' she added as an afterthought. 'Anna approved it.'

'Then we get you a new one and you change here.'

She sighed longingly. 'That would be lovely. No tassels. No heirloom furniture. This place feels like home already.'

He laughed. 'Then let's do it.'

She sat up with a wild splash. She was so tempted, but she didn't believe they could do it. '*Could* we? The time . . . '

'I'll make some calls. There's got to be a dress you'd like somewhere in Liburno.'

'Actually, I already know one.'

Jonas beamed. 'The universe is providing. Get your coat.'

They found the boutique eventually after a few false starts and identified a dress that Jonas said was sufficiently dryad-like in shimmery bronze and green and gold. Then, to the shop assistant's delight, they rushed out into a taxi with their purchase, hand in hand, giggling.

They dressed in Jonas's bedroom, doing up each other's hard-to-reach buttons.

'I hope you enjoy *this* ball,' said Jonas. 'Though you probably hate all princessing by now.'

Hope was indignant. 'I don't hate princessing. I haven't done any princessing. Actually, I think I might quite enjoy some of it. The stuff with kids, for instance. But not full-time. And in my own way, not Anna's.'

His eyes gleamed. 'Like swinging down ropes to rescue a subject?'

They choked, picturing the immaculate crown princess on a forest assault course.

'And I'm not wasting all that blasted folk dancing.'

'Good thinking.' He patted his Hussar's jacket and surveyed his image with satisfaction. 'No sword.'

'What?'

'Can't wear a sword for folk dancing. God bless it.' He looked at her, twisting her red curls on top of her head. 'Leave it loose,' he said huskily. 'I can watch it gleaming in the candlelight across a crowded room.

Hope chuckled and gave up on the elaborate hairstyle with relief. She kissed him and didn't manage any make-up at all.

★ ★ ★

The ballroom was already full: of women in gorgeous gowns; men in elaborate uniforms or elegant dinner jackets; crystal chandeliers like a thousand stars; floor-to-ceiling Venetian mirrors, reflecting the crowd in unending repetition; an orchestra playing lilting music; the clink of glasses, the buzz of conversation . . .

Jonas took Hope's hand and stepped through the great gilded double doors and looked down at the gorgeous kaleidoscope. Hope gulped. The buzz rose to a crescendo and then slowly died away. The conductor brought the orchestra to a concluding cadence. Everyone stared up at them.

He grinned at her. 'Here we go, my dryad. Folk dancing is only minutes away.

And as she was laughing delightedly, he led her to stand at the top of the staircase, looked down at his guests and said, 'Welcome, all, to this — my happiest of birthdays. Allow me to present Miss Hope Kennard, who has done me the honour to consent to become my wife. Darling Hope, welcome to San Michele.'

We do hope that you have enjoyed reading this large print book.

Did you know that all of our titles are available for purchase?

We publish a wide range of high quality large print books including:
Romances, Mysteries, Classics
General Fiction
Non Fiction and Westerns

Special interest titles available in large print are:
The Little Oxford Dictionary
Music Book, Song Book
Hymn Book, Service Book

Also available from us courtesy of Oxford University Press:
Young Readers' Dictionary
(large print edition)
Young Readers' Thesaurus
(large print edition)

For further information or a free brochure, please contact us at:
Ulverscroft Large Print Books Ltd.,
The Green, Bradgate Road, Anstey,
Leicester, LE7 7FU, England.
Tel: (00 44) **0116 236 4325**
Fax: (00 44) **0116 234 0205**

BLUEPRINT FOR LOVE

Henriette Gyland

Hazel Dobson is pleased when she gets temp work at Gough Associates, an architectural company based in a beautiful manor house in Norfolk. While it's a far cry from the bright lights of London, she is keen to get away from a mundane job with a lecherous boss, and to spend some time with her great-aunt. There she meets handsome and wealthy Jonathan Gough, and sees a chance at happiness and a family with him. But some people just don't want Hazel and Jonathan to be happy . . .

LAKELAND INTERLUDE

Jean M. Long

Following a painful break-up, Casey Brett decides to start a new life in the Lake District as an assistant in her friend Flora's Dance and Drama Studio. But it's not all plain sailing, as a fellow instructor feels Casey is stepping on her toes, she receives the unwanted romantic attentions of a local hiking guide, and she loses several of her most promising students. But she also meets wealthy businessman Blake Lawley, and feels an instant frisson. Can Casey overcome her problems and find happiness in her new home?

THE TIME OF THE FLOOD

Miranda Barnes

The Northumbrian village of Carlton is hit by unprecedented flooding when torrential rain overwhelms its defences and the river bursts its banks. During a long and difficult night, Anna Mason and her friend David Wilson work together to help the needy. Meanwhile, moody Gregory McKenzie, the attractive visiting grandson of one of the villagers, shows a previously unsuspected side to his character. But the flood will also wash away decades of secrecy, unearthing old family mysteries . . .

THE GHOST OF GLENDALE

Natalie Kleinman

Phoebe Marcham is resigned to spinsterhood, unwilling to settle for less than the deep love her parents shared. Then adventurer Duncan Armstrong rides into her home wood, with laughter in his eyes and more charm in his little finger than anyone she has ever met before. Far from ridiculing her family ghost, Duncan resolves to help solve the mystery that has left Simon Marcham a soul in torment for two hundred years. Will they be able to put the ghost to rest — and find love together?

THE WEDDING REJECT TABLE

Angela Britnell

When Maggie Taylor, a cake decorator, and Chad Robertson, a lawyer from Nashville, meet at a wedding in Cornwall, it's not under the best circumstances. They have both been assigned to 'the reject table' alongside a toxic collection of grumpy great-aunts, bitter divorcées and stuffy organists. Maggie has grown used to being the reject, though when Chad helps her out of a wedding cake disaster she begins to wonder whether the future could hold more for her. But will Chad be strong enough to deal with the other problems in Maggie's life?